Rose Mellie Rose

European Women Writers Series

University of Nebraska Press: Lincoln & London

ROSE
MELLIE
ROSE

with 'The Story of the Triptych' by

Marie Redonnet

TRANSLATED BY

JORDAN STUMP

Originally published as *Rose Mélie
Rose* © copyright
1987 by Les Éditions de Minuit
Translation © 1994
by the University of Nebraska Press
All rights reserved
Manufactured in the United States
of America. The paper in
this book meets the minimum re-
quirements of American
National Standard for Information
Sciences – Permanence
of Paper for Printed Library Mater-
ials, ANSI Z39.48-1984.
Library of Congress Cataloging-in-
Publication Data
Redonnet, Marie. [Rose Mélie Rose.
English] Rose Mellie
Rose / by Marie Redonnet; trans-
lated by Jordan Stump.
p. cm. – (European women writers
series) ISBN 0-8032-8952-9
I. Title. II. Series. PQ2678.E285R67
1995 843'.914 – dc20 94-1313 CIP

Contents

Rose Mellie Rose

The black rocks beside the river are made of quartz, like
the sand. Rose says the light is stronger here than anywhere else because of the properties of the quartz. It must
have gradually burned her eyes over the years. She squints
all the time. Her eyesight is becoming worse and worse. It
is as if she had lost the strength to see. At the end of the
river are the falls. After the falls, the river disappears. The
noise of the falls is so loud you can't hear anything else. I
have always lived near the falls. Everything is white where
the falls are because of the foam. Sometimes you can see
the rainbow in the middle of the falls. Rose says she never
sees the rainbow anymore.

I like to go up and down the river. I know all the rocks.
The rocks are slippery, you have to be careful when you
jump. I have been jumping from one rock to another for
so long now it's like a game to me. The farther down the
river you go, the higher the banks are. I never go any
farther than where the banks start to rise. I have to give
myself time to get back to the falls. Rose would worry if I
was not back by the time the sun sets. Beyond the falls, it's
the mountains. Rose has never been farther than the falls.

The region used to be full of little sawmills powered by
the river. There were many woodcutters in the forest sur-
rounding the falls. You still find cabins that the woodcutters abandoned. I don't like the forest, except for the cabins. The forest is always dark and cold, even in summer.
The road starts at the falls. Rose says the road runs the

length of the forest and continues down to Oât. Oât is the port where they load the wood. The road was built a long time ago for the trucks that transport the wood. But the wood from the forest doesn't sell anymore. So the sawmills are closing, the woodcutters are leaving, and the road is no longer kept up because the trucks have stopped coming up to the falls.

Rose says the river disappears under the mountain, where its source is. The river comes up from underground in front of the grotto, a little before the falls. It is a well-known site. It has always attracted travelers. When I was little, I called the grotto the Fairy Grotto, after the title of a legend in my book. The legend says that newlyweds who go and spend their wedding night in the Fairy Grotto have a child nine months later. The legend also says than when a traveler feels his last moments approaching he goes and takes refuge in the Fairy Grotto. When he dies, the fairies take away his body. There are fewer and fewer travelers coming up to the falls. The book of legends is the only book Rose owned. It was the book she taught me to read from. It is my book now. Rose gave it to me as a reward for having learned to read so well. It was written in the old alphabet. Rose can only read the old alphabet. It is the only alphabet I know too.

Rose discovered me one morning in the grotto. I had just been born. Rose lives in the only house in the area of the falls. It's a wooden house, still in good condition. Rose says the wood from the forest no longer sells because people have stopped building houses of wood. She called her house the Hermitage. The Hermitage is also the name of the site. Rose turned her house into a souvenir shop. That was a good idea. The travelers who come up to the falls and who go to see the grotto buy a souvenir of the Hermitage. Rose had moved to the falls a little before she found me in the grotto. She was already old. Rose has been old as long as I have known her. She would not have given up her souvenir shop for anything in the world.

Rose is even older now. She says she doesn't know what her age is anymore. She must be very old. She is so old that I don't know what her age could be either. She is stooped and wrinkled. She can scarcely see at all now. She has difficulty walking, and leans on her stick. She moves more and more awkwardly. She doesn't want to admit it, and she walks through the shop as if she could see perfectly well. The souvenirs are valuable and fragile. When I see Rose in the shop with her stick, I am afraid something will happen to the souvenirs. I am the one who runs the shop. Rose does nothing but wait for travelers to come. She has to wait longer and longer between travelers. People must be forgetting about the site. Rose says she will close the shop when her last souvenir is sold. She says it will soon be time for me to leave the falls.

When Rose found me in the grotto, I had nothing. She has always said she hadn't seen anyone come up to the grotto for several days before that. She named me Mellie because she thinks Mellie is the most beautiful name, along with Rose. She did not register me at the municipal offices, because the municipal offices are in Oât and Oât is several days from the falls. Rose has never been back to Oât since she moved to the Hermitage. She has always said that what matters is not for me to be registered at the municipal offices of Oât, but for me to be named Mellie.

What had to happen happened. Rose broke the last souvenirs. She hit the table with her stick. The table was very fragile, and it gave way. All the souvenirs were lined up on the table, and they were all breakable. Rose asked me to pick up the souvenirs and to go throw the pieces into the river. When the souvenirs reach the bottom of the falls they won't be in pieces any more, but in particles. Rose seems relieved that there are no more souvenirs to sell.

When I came back from throwing the broken souvenirs into the river, Rose told me that it was time for me to leave the Hermitage. I didn't believe her. So she told me her last moments were approaching. She has known it since her stick hit the table holding her last souvenirs. She wants to spend her last night alone in the grotto. She has always lived with her book of legends. She wants to finish her life like in the legend. When she told me goodbye, she was already drifting away. She said now I can live without her, far from the Hermitage. The Hermitage is only a temporary stop. She lived there for twelve years like me, her last twelve years and my first twelve years. I saw her climb the path that leads to the grotto. Her hair was undone. I noticed that it was long and very white. She always kept it hidden under her bonnet. I watched her climb as if she were someone else.

The next morning, I climbed up to the grotto. Rose was dead. I closed her eyes. I stayed beside her for a long time, looking at her. At noon, when the sunlight came in, it lit up Rose. She seemed to be sleeping. It was as if she were not dead. I buried her in the grotto, where she found me twelve years ago. It makes a good shelter. I carved her name into the wall, and mine too. And then I drew a line between them. It says Rose and Mellie on the wall of the grotto.

Rose died on my birthday. I am twelve years old, counting from the day Rose found me in the grotto. I saw the blood on my sheets as soon as I woke up. This is my first period. It came on my twelfth birthday, which is also the day of Rose's death. Rose told me it would be coming soon. She could see it from my body, which has changed a great deal over the past year. She explained to me what you have to do when you have your first period, as if she already knew she would not be there. She told me I would have to leave the Hermitage the day I had my first period. She knew how to recognize the omens. She saw them everywhere, even with her bad eyesight. I have never seen an omen myself. Rose said it was normal not to see them at my age. Now that Rose is dead and I am having my first period, I have to leave. I have to obey Rose, even if she is no longer here. It must be an omen that I am having my first period on my twelfth birthday, which is also the day of Rose's death.

Rose had written an address on the last page of my book of legends. That is where I have to go. Rose did not leave me empty-handed, she left me an address. On the last page of the book of legends, she wrote: 7 Charms Street, in Oât. It is unmistakably Rose's handwriting. Oât is at the end of the road. All I have to do to get to Oât is follow the road.

Before I left, I took down the sign. Rose never said what I should do with the sign. I don't want to leave it hanging up over the front door now that Rose is dead and I am leaving for Oât. It's a tiny sign. It has Souvenir Shop engraved on it in the old alphabet. The sign attracted travelers to the souvenir shop even though it was so small. How would Rose have lived without her shop? The souvenirs sold well. I never lacked for anything at the Hermitage. Rose wanted me to have everything I need.

I am going to leave the door of the Hermitage unlocked. I can't lock it because Rose lost the key a few days ago. I hope travelers will keep coming up to the falls, even now that the souvenir shop is closed and Rose is dead. I am going to leave everything in place, just as Rose left it. Rose never told me about her life before the Hermitage. And yet she had a long life before she came to the falls. She only lived at the Hermitage for twelve years, with me.

Before that, she lived in Oât. Oât is the only place she ever knew, along with the Hermitage.

§2

I put my belongings in my bag, along with some provisions for the trip, the sign from the Hermitage – it really is a tiny sign, since it can fit into my bag – and my book of legends. That was all I could fit into my bag. The sign is my only souvenir of the Hermitage. It isn't a souvenir like the others, since it was never for sale. I didn't want to take one last look at the grotto or even the falls. I turned my back to them and did not look behind me.

This is the first time I have taken the road down the hill. Until now I always followed the river down. It really isn't a road anymore since the trucks have stopped using it. All I see is trees in front of me and around me. I am getting deeper and deeper into the forest, where I have never been. I am walking as quickly as I can in spite of the pains in my stomach. Rose told me I might have pains in my stomach during my first period. But I never thought it would hurt this much. My underwear is stained and wet. And yet I did everything just as Rose explained. I am sure I'm going to stain my dress too. It is not pleasant to walk with wet underwear, especially if it's wet with blood. Periods are painful and uncomfortable, and even more so when you have a long walk ahead of you.

I stopped in a woodcutter's cabin, just before nightfall. I was lucky to find one so near the road. The cabin protects me from the forest. I put my fingers in my ears to shut out the noises of the forest. They scare me now that I can no 8 longer hear the noise of the falls. I put on clean underwear. It was nice not to feel wet. This is my first trip. Fortunately, I fell asleep quickly. Otherwise I would have felt afraid all alone in the cabin in the middle of the forest. A dream woke me up. In my dream, I saw Rose in a wedding dress. She was very young, and I did not recognize her. I was holding her veil and crying like I have never cried before. It makes me feel funny not to have recognized Rose. I do not feel any grief over her death. It was only in my dream that I was crying, but I was not crying because Rose was dead.

I went back to the road and walked for another day without meeting anyone. The woodcutters have all left and the sawmills are closed. There is no traffic on the road. I still walk quickly in spite of the pains in my stomach and now in my legs as well. I am not used to walking so quickly or for so long. My underwear is wet again. The blood started flowing again as soon as I got back to the road. The road never stops going downhill. The forest is impenetrable. I hear the river in the distance, but I can't see it. I slept in a woodcutter's cabin like the first night and I dreamt about Rose again. This time I was not there to hold her veil. She was only wearing her wedding gown and she was still as young as before, but she was dead. The forest is giving me these bad dreams. I never dreamt about Rose at the Hermitage. Rose died very old, and not very young like in my dream. I don't even know if she had ever been married. She did not wear a wedding ring on her finger. If she had been married, she would have had a wedding ring. You would think Rose had no past before the Hermitage.

On the third day, I was exhausted from walking. Oât is farther than I thought. I have eaten all my provisions and I have run out of strength. I told myself I would never make it to the end of the road. That was when I saw a little sawmill with a yellow truck just in front of it. So I am saved, I will not die of hunger and exhaustion on the road to Oât. The driver was loading his truck. I asked him if he could take me to Oât. He looked at me as if I were an apparition. This must be the first time he has ever seen a girl walking along the road from the falls. He began to laugh. He said there was nothing he would like better than to take me to Oât. His yellow truck is brand-new and covered with chrome that has been polished until it shines.

Finally, the driver told me to get into the cab. It's time to go. The seat was so soft I sank into it. The driver is not curious. He didn't ask me what I was doing on the road or where I was coming from. He is still recovering from his surprise at seeing me coming down the road. And now here I am sitting next to him in the cab of his truck. He must surely not meet many people on the road that runs through the forest, as deserted as it is nowadays. He turned on the radio. This is the first time I have ever heard a radio. It's very loud, much louder than the falls. The driver told me it was in stereo. He showed me the two speakers where the sound comes from. That's what makes you feel so surrounded by the sound, because it comes out of two speakers at the same time. I am in a daze, the music from the radio, the heat in the truck. The driver turned on the heat just for the pleasure of pushing the buttons and showing me that everything works. He even offered me a cigarette so he could use the cigarette lighter. The dashboard is covered with buttons. The driver says this truck is the most advanced model, and he bought it with his savings. I told him I had never smoked cigarettes before. He laughed again. I felt sick to my stomach after my first cigarette. I am embarrassed to find that my underwear is wet again. I am sure it's going to stain the brand-new seat cover in the truck. The driver opened the window to get rid of the cigarette smoke. The air came into the cab all of a sudden. I gasped for breath. My head is spinning from being in the truck for the first time. There are turns on the road. The driver takes them roughly. And there are jolts in the truck because of the potholes. The driver can brag about the suspension of his truck, but I still feel the jolts in my stomach. The driver does not know what it feels like to have your period for the first time. He turned the radio up even louder. He beats time with his hands on the steering wheel. He asked me how old I was. I told him I had just turned twelve years old and had my first period. He laughed at the coincidence. He stares at me insistently as he drives and beats time with his hands. I feel a little faint. Things look blurry. The driver seems nice. Night began to fall. The driver turned his lights on, first the parking lights and then the headlights. Time passes quickly in the cab of the truck. The headlights are so powerful they light up the whole road. I hardly recognize the forest lit up by the truck's headlights. We drove for a long time in the dark through the forest.

Suddenly the truck left the forest. I saw lights in the distance, and on either side of the road I saw water. I thought it was the ocean. The driver told me it was only the lagoon. Before the ocean there is a lagoon, and between the two is Oât. The lights in the distance are the lights of Oât. The driver stopped his truck on the shoulder of the road. The lagoon looks enormous in the dark. The driver turned off the headlights and switched on the dome light in the cab. He turned down the radio. He began to caress me through my dress. His hands move slowly. That was the first thing I noticed, and then the pleasure I felt at being caressed through my dress by the truck driver. He whispered in my ear that this was another thing that had to happen. The best time would be during my first period. Then he lowered the seatback. He had not told me the seat could be made into a bunk. Just pushing a button hidden under the seat lowers the seatback to make a bunk. It really is an ultramodern truck. It feels nice to stretch out. My stomach pains are not so bad now. The driver pressed himself against me. He put his hand in my underwear. It doesn't bother him that I am having my period. He took off my underwear, and then my dress too. And he went on caressing me. It isn't the same now that he has taken off my dress. There is blood on the driver's hands and also on me where he caressed me. The driver said I was well-developed for a twelve-year-old. That was what Rose said too. But Rose never talked to me about truck drivers on the road, probably because they never come up to the falls. There is a blood stain on the bunk where I was sitting before.

The truck driver kept caressing me. I let him go on. I did everything like the truck driver wanted. I want to let him go on. The driver took me gently without hurting me. On the bunk, the blood mixed with the blood. The driver said I am not shy and that it's good to be with me on the bunk in his truck. I told him that I also thought it was good to be with him on the bunk in his truck. It's warm in the cab, there is music on the radio. My stomach pains are gone. I don't feel faint anymore.

The truck driver started up the engine again and got back on the road. I pushed the button. The bunk became a seat again, and I got dressed. I threw my wet underwear out the window. I looked at the lagoon. My underwear fell into the lagoon. The night is ending. Suddenly the road became paved. The needle on the speedometer jumped up to seventy. The driver said he likes to go fast. His truck is made to go fast, not to crawl along the road through the forest. He also says his sawmill is not like it used to be, it doesn't make money anymore. He is preoccupied by the low demand for wood. But just after that, he said he would always get by with his truck. I must have dozed a little.

I am not a virgin anymore. Rose never told me I should stay a virgin. After the lagoon, it's Oât. The driver explained the unique thing about Oât. It has had two ports, one after the other. The first port was built on the lagoon. It was an inland port. They built piers on the lagoon, and the ships loaded the wood there. The ships followed a channel to get to the ocean. The channel linked the ocean with the lagoon. But the channel became filled in with sand little by little, until it was no longer navigable. That was when they built the seaport, for the ships that couldn't get to the lagoon. Now the inland port is gone. The lagoon is spreading. It has covered the piers of the old port. Oât is in two parts now, the seaport and the city built behind the lagoon in the days of the old port. The city has been in decline since they built the seaport. There are fewer and fewer ships in the port because the demand for wood is falling off. The seaport is also in decline. The driver says he doesn't see what good it did to build it. There are fewer and fewer people in Oât. I told the driver I was going to 7 Charms Street. The driver only knows the port. He says driving is impossible in the city because the streets are too narrow. He has never heard of Charms Street. He turned onto the boulevard. It's the main boulevard leading to the port. He left me at the side of the boulevard. He pointed me in the direction of the city off in the distance, on the other side of the vacant land. He gave me his address. He told me not to forget to register at the municipal offices of the port. All newcomers have to register there. The municipal offices are at the end of the boulevard, in the Customs building. The driver told me to ask for Miss Martha, the head of the reception center.

The ocean is directly in front of me. It's rough and very blue. It does not look like the lagoon. The truck driver wrote his address in an alphabet I don't know. It must be the new alphabet. I can't read the driver's address. I will have to learn the new alphabet now that I am going to live in Oât. My book of legends talks about the ocean constantly. I see white birds, much bigger than the birds in the forest, flying in circles around the big ship anchored at the end of the pier. They must be seagulls. The driver stopped his truck at the end of the pier in front of the big ship. In my book of legends, seagulls sometimes follow a river to its source. I never saw seagulls at the Hermitage, maybe because the falls make too much noise. The ocean is rough, but it is still much quieter than the falls. The sky seems bigger and bluer by the ocean. My period is over. I did the right thing throwing my wet underwear out the window of the truck. I am not at the Hermitage anymore, but in Oât. And now that I have had my first period and I am not a virgin anymore, I am a young girl.

§3

The vacant land begins just on the other side of the boulevard. It must rain a lot in Oât. The vacant land is flooded
along one side. The water is standing stagnant there. I
asked for directions to Charms Street. It is the next one
after Steps Street. I am on Steps Street. It's a narrow street
with houses squeezed up against each other. Their wooden
facades are deteriorating. Many of the houses seem to be
closed up. The one pleasant surprise is that the names of
the streets are written in the old alphabet. Steps Street is
very quiet, it feels abandoned. Charms Street is just after
Steps Street. It's a wider street with bigger houses. The
wood of the facades is varnished, but the varnish needs to
be redone. There are balconies in front of the windows.
The shutters are closed, except at number 7. So number 7
is still lived in. I saw the sign as soon as I looked up. It's the
only sign on Charms Street, and I did not see any signs on
Steps Street. The sign says Souvenir Shop in the old alphabet. There is a knocker on the door. I knocked several
times before a very old man came and opened the door. He
is bundled up in a dressing gown that looks so old it has
lost all its color. I told him I had come from the Hermitage
and that Rose sent me. He is deaf, he can scarcely hear
what I say. Then I had the idea of getting the sign from the
Hermitage out of my bag. He took the sign, he looked at it
attentively, and he let me into his house.

The house is very dark. One end of the hallway opens
onto a little courtyard with a flowering tree in the middle.

The old man opened a door and told me this would be my room. It's a tiny room, almost a child's room, with a narrow bed, a writing desk, and a bookshelf. The window looks onto the courtyard. The old man told me his name, he is called Nem. He called me Rose. I told him my name was Mellie, not Rose. He says that this is Rose's house, not Nem's house. Rose used to live in this house, before Nem lived in it. Nem has only lived in it for twelve years, since the library closed. Nem was the librarian of Oât. He says he heard a great deal about Rose but never met her. Rose never came to the library and Nem never left the library. When the library closed, Nem heard that Rose's house was vacant. That was when he had the idea of moving into it. He wanted to show me around the whole house. The rooms on the ground floor are empty. The sign is deceptive, there is no souvenir shop at 7 Charms Street. It's full of dust and spider webs. The wood is mildewed. Upstairs too, the rooms are empty and the wood is mildewed. There are many rooms in Rose's house. Nem says the Charms neighborhood was very fashionable in the days of the inland port. Nem's room is above my room, with a little balcony overlooking the courtyard. You can only see the top of the tree, like a bouquet of pink flowers. The bookshelf is full of big books. I have never seen such big books. My book of legends looks tiny next to them. In front of the balcony there is a writing desk with notebooks as big as the books.

Nem saw that I was looking at the big books. He gave

me one to look through. It's written in the old alphabet, but it looks nothing like the old alphabet Rose taught me. Nem says it is an older alphabet that did not originate in Oât. He doesn't know where it comes from. He found the big books in a crate at the very back of the storage area in the library. The crate had never been opened. Nem kept his discovery to himself. When the library closed and he moved to 7 Charms Street, he took his crate with him. Since then, he has devoted all his time to studying the books. He began by deciphering the unknown alphabet. Then he translated all the books in the crate. He translated them into the old alphabet of Oât. The big notebooks piled up on the writing desk are the translations of the books. Nem should be happy to have finished his translations, but he isn't. He says he has realized all of a sudden that he deciphered the alphabet incorrectly. He says he cannot imagine how he could have deciphered it incorrectly. He says his mistake was using the old alphabet of Oât as a model. It was not the right model. He got off on the wrong track. He says he works slower than time, when he needs to go faster than time to decipher the alphabet. Nem says understanding time and deciphering the alphabet are the same thing. I don't understand any of what Nem is telling me. He says he is losing his faculties and his memory. He says he wasted his time as the librarian of Oât. Now he is not competent and he is too old. It's too late. His life is ending just when it should be beginning. He would like to be my age, twelve years old. He says twelve years old is just the age to be able to begin things.

Walking back down the hall, I noticed a photograph hanging on the wall. It is a photograph of a young girl. It's blurry and yellowed. There is nothing written on the photo. Nem says it is a photograph of Rose. But he has never seen Rose. The old Rose did not look anything like that photo. Nem hooked a device up to his ears so he could hear me better. The device looks very used and it crackles in Nem's ears. It's not easy to have a conversation with Nem, even when he has his device on, because the crackling prevents him from hearing. I told him Rose was dead. He told me he knew. There is no way he can know that. What he knows is something else. When he says Rose, it is as if he had said all there was to say. He repeats that it is getting late. He says Rose's house is not what he thought it would be.

Nem left me alone, and I could finally move into my room. I took my things out of my bag. Nem kept the sign from the Hermitage. My room lacks something without my sign. I was so exhausted from the trip that I fell asleep without realizing it. I could never have predicted such a sudden and complete change in the way I live. When I woke up, Nem was sitting on a low chair in the courtyard just in front of my window. The sun is setting. I slept for a long time. Nem rests in his courtyard every evening before night falls. He knocked on my window when he saw I was awake. I opened the window. The smell of the lagoon came into my room. I don't like that smell. Nem told me about Mellie, his old servant. She died when the library closed. Nem misses her very much, he says she is irreplaceable. It's because his servant is dead that Rose's house is so badly kept up and that there is dust everywhere. Nem also told me about his nearest neighbor, whose name is Mellie like his old servant. Mellie lives on Charms Way just behind Charms Street. She is the one who takes care of Nem and his house. All the houses on Charms Street are vacant now except Nem's. Nem says Mellie is not like his servant even though she has the same name. She doesn't know how to keep up Rose's house. Nem told me Mellie is eager for me to visit her. I asked Nem for a map of Oât. He told me you don't need a map to know your way around Oât. Oât was built without any sort of plan, first behind the lagoon and now along the boulevard leading to the port. He says the Charms neighborhood is the most beautiful. He talked a great deal about Wardens Square. It is just at the edge of the Charms neighborhood, but it's not a part of it. In the old days all the municipal buildings of Oât were clustered around Wardens Square. They closed one after another. The library was the last to close. Nem lived in Wardens Square for a long time. Before he was the librarian of Oât, he lived on Markers Street, which runs along the lagoon. He says Markers Street has been uninhabitable for a long time. He says the lagoon neighborhood is becoming more and more uninhabitable because of flooding. The Charms neighborhood and Wardens Square are floodproof. Nem says he is not sure if moving into Rose's house was the right thing for him to do. It is no one's house since Rose left. He says leaving was the right thing for her to do. Now that he is no longer the librarian of Oât, Nem says he is no one.

My moving into the house has not changed Nem's life at all. He was very hospitable, but he doesn't want to know anything about me. He has not even asked what I am going to do in Oât. He goes to bed when it gets dark. The electrical system is not working. The switches don't turn anything on. I have to use a candle to see, just like at the Hermitage. Rose never told me about this house. Still, she wrote the address on the last page of the book of legends. She never told me about Oât either. I feel comfortable in this room. The candles light up the whole room, not just my bedside like at the Hermitage. Before I went to sleep, I reread The Queen of the Fairies. It's a very mysterious legend. The Queen of the Fairies has been missing forever and the fairies look for her without ever having seen her. Rose used to say there were several versions of the legend. There is only one in my book. I am happy the truck driver gave me his address, even though I can't read it because I don't know the new alphabet yet. I have not forgotten how much I owe the driver. Thanks to him, I am not a virgin anymore. It's bad enough not knowing the new alphabet and not being registered at the municipal offices, all I needed was to come to Oât a virgin. I can see the yellow truck as if it were right in front of me, and the cab with the seat that turned into a bunk. The driver will have a hard time washing the blood stain out of the seat cover. It will probably always be a little stained. Thanks to the stain, the driver will not forget me.

§4

I heard hammering when I woke up. It was Nem up on his ladder, taking down the sign. He says it is high time it was taken down, since the letters are beginning to rust away. From close up, the Charms Street sign doesn't look like the one from the Hermitage. The Hermitage sign is intact, it isn't rusting away. Nem says this is the day the secondhand man comes by. He is going to sell him the sign for a good price. The secondhand man has been coveting it for years. The secondhand man has already bought all the signs in the Charms neighborhood. He has been waiting a long time for Nem to sell him his, so he could say he had finally bought them all. The secondhand man had already bought everything that was in Rose's house. So the rooms are empty because the secondhand man took everything away. All of a sudden, Nem thought of my sign from the Hermitage. He went to get it right away and he looked at it for a long time. I was afraid he would want to put it up where the one he had just taken down was. But no, he gave it back to me. He told me the secondhand man would pay a great deal of money to have my sign. He has spent a lot of time looking all over the Charms neighborhood for a sign exactly like mine. Selling my sign to the secondhand man is out of the question. It's my only souvenir from the Hermitage and it is not for sale. Nem's face fell. He went back up to his room without saying anything. He must have been thinking about his alphabet again, and about time moving faster than he is.

I took the truck driver's address to show to Miss Martha as a letter of introduction, and I set off towards the port. I was surprised by the crisp sea air. The sea air doesn't come into the city, which faces the lagoon. I walked up the boulevard to the municipal offices. The municipal offices really are in the Customs building. They do not seem very large. There is a glassed-in office at the entrance to the hallway. I told the attendant I had come to see Miss Martha. She pointed the way to the reception center at the end of the hall. It's not a real office. They must not receive many newcomers. I waited a long time for Miss Martha. The municipal offices seem empty. Miss Martha came out with a hurried look, as if I were disturbing her. Right away she asked me what boat I had come in on. She thought there were no boats scheduled to arrive from the continent today. I didn't even have time to show my surprise before Miss Martha told me there was no room for me in Oât. All the places are taken. When I finally got a chance to talk, I told her right away that she was wrong about me. I didn't come by boat like she thinks, but by the road that leads to the forest. And I don't come from the continent, but from the falls. Miss Martha looked at me with amazement. I took the opportunity to explain the whole situation and to tell her about the truck driver. While I was talking, she took the address I showed her, she looked at it and she put it in her pocket. Then finally she smiled at me and said this really is the first time she has seen a case like mine. She says Rose was wrong not to register me at the municipal offices of Oât. Twelve years ago, the municipal offices of the port had just opened. They would have investigated. Miss Martha says Rose may have taken me in by mistake. Now it is too late to investigate. Miss Martha wants me to register Rose's death at the office of records. That is the glassed-in office at the entrance to the hallway. Miss Martha says Rose must have a death certificate on file, just as I should have had a birth certificate on file twelve years ago.

Next Miss Martha wanted to make me an identity card. I cannot live in Oât without an identity card. She made me a temporary identity card. On the card she wrote Mellie, and next to Mellie a number. I didn't understand about the number, and I asked her what it meant. It is in place of my last name, which is unknown. Mellie is not my full name, it is only my first name. Miss Martha said the number is the same thing as the last name to the municipal offices. Mellie is not enough to identify me, because there are a lot of Mellies in Oât. But my number is unique, it's 3175. I have to know it by heart. She asked me to come back with a photo, and then she can make me my permanent identity card. I told her I don't have a photo because I have never been photographed. Miss Martha gave me the address of the photographer, 1 Storks Street. I have to tell the photographer that Miss Martha sent me. He has not taken any photos for a long time, but he will make an exception for me if Miss Martha sends me.

I took advantage of Miss Martha's kindness to ask how I can learn the new alphabet. Miss Martha was very interested when I told her I knew the old alphabet. Right away she told me about her project, which she can't see to completion because she doesn't know the old alphabet. She wants to open a library in the municipal offices. But no one can read the books from the old library of Oât anymore, because they are written in the old alphabet. If I learn the new alphabet I will be able to translate the books and Miss Martha will be able to open her library. She says it is a good sign that I live in Nem's house, since Nem used to be the librarian of Oât. She says Nem caused the downfall of the library by refusing to learn the new alphabet. Miss Martha wants to save the library from disappearing. She says she is counting on me to help her. No one my age could ever expect to be hired as a translator in the municipal offices. First I have to learn the new alphabet. Miss Martha gave me a series of pamphlets to learn from. It is a method she developed while she was training to be a teacher. But the school closed just before she finished her studies. The school is on the continent now. Miss Martha did not want to leave Oât, so she never became a teacher.

She was hired at the municipal offices, which had just opened. I am her first pupil. She told me she would correct my exercises. Rose never told me I was living on an island. Oât is also the name of the island. Rose never told me about the continent either. Does that change everything that Oât is an island and not the continent?

Miss Martha told me I had to go to the clinic for a medical examination. The clinic is part of the hospital. That's the big white villa you pass as you come down the boulevard. You can't tell it is a hospital. Miss Martha personally oversees the operation of the clinic. Every traveler coming from the continent has to undergo a medical examination. That is a rule of the city of Oât. Miss Martha says it is imperative that Oât be protected from the diseases of the continent. The diseases of the continent are her obsession. Oât's population is declining because of emigration to the continent. They must not let the remaining population of Oât be decimated by the diseases of the continent. Miss Martha has more than the reception center on her mind. She wants to open a library, and she sees to it that the municipal laws are observed. She says a seaport is always a good environment for the spread of disease. So far, thanks to the required medical examinations, Oât has been spared and the people live to a very old age. I don't see what disease I could have caught at the falls. But Miss Martha allows no exceptions to the rule. And the municipal law makes no distinction between the continent and the falls.

I went back down the boulevard to the fishing port. The boulevard runs from the fishing port to the Customs building. The seaport never really got started because of the bad market for wood. It was built just at the wrong time. The dinghies are squeezed up against each other along the piers of the fishing port. Oât lives mostly on fishing now. There is just one fishing boat in the middle of all the dinghies. It's a tiny boat compared to the big ship I saw when I arrived in Oât, but next to the dinghies it looks like a real boat. I sat down on the dock in front of the boat. I tell myself that the continent is over there, but all I can see is water. So it is as if the continent didn't exist. The dinghies are old. The boat is old too, but its name is freshly painted. It's written in the new alphabet.

A young fisherman sat down on the next dock over. He has just come out of the boat. He carries his meal in his bag, and he offered half to me. He told me his name is Yem. I asked him if he had ever been to the continent. He has never been there and has no desire to go. I have no desire to go there either. Yem is sixteen. He is big for his age. I am big for my age too. Yem says this is the first time a girl has come and sat down on the dock in front of his boat. I asked him to read me the name of his boat. It is the Queen of the Fairies. I don't recognize the name written in the new alphabet on Yem's boat. And yet it is a name I know well, since it is the title of one of the legends in my book. It's strange how a name changes between the old alphabet and the new. You would never think it was the same name. Yem is proud to work on his boat. The skipper of the Queen of the Fairies is teaching him everything he needs to know. Yem lives in the little cabin just under the deck. He says he was born on a boat that left here a long time ago. This is the first time he hasn't wanted to change to another boat. Until now, every boat tempted him. He offered to show me around the Queen of the Fairies next time I came and sat on the dock. Today, there is no time. Yem's eyes are the color of the ocean. I told him I came from the falls. He doesn't know about the falls. All he knows of Oât is the port. I told him I was born in a grotto. He was born on a boat and I was born in a grotto. It's not the same thing. The skipper of the Queen of the Fairies came along. Yem went with him, and said he would see me soon. I will come back and sit on the dock again. I want to see Yem's boat. I forgot to tell him his boat has the same name as the legend in my book. Only the alphabets are different.

§5

I did not dare ask Miss Martha to give me back the truck driver's address. But it annoys me that she didn't give it back. Nem didn't come downstairs to open the door for me when I knocked, even though I knocked very loudly. So I decided to go and visit Mellie. You would almost think that Charms Way was Charms Street, except that the street sign says Way instead of Street. There is only one house whose shutters are open. It is the same house as

Nem's, with varnished wood and balconies. Now that Nem has taken down the sign, it would be impossible to tell the two houses apart if one were not on Charms Street and the other on Charms Way. Mellie came and opened the door as soon as I knocked. She is at least as old as Nem. But she likes to have visitors. She told me to come in right away, without even asking who I am. She is not deaf like Nem. I don't need to shout when I talk to her. She is coquettish for her age. She wears a pearl-gray embroidered woolen dress with a matching shawl and pretty shoes that also match, and a bonnet that looks like Rose's. She told me right away that she was very happy I was named Mellie like her. She didn't think anyone was named Mellie anymore. She told me I was welcome in her house. She lives cut off from everything now. She says Nem is not really a neighbor, that he is too out of the way in the middle of the Charms neighborhood.

Mellie wanted to show me around her house. The inside is nothing like Nem's house. There are lamps burning everywhere even though it's daytime. Mellie explains that it is because she has the beginnings of a cataract. There is a thin veil over everything she sees. The veil seems to disappear when she stands near a lamp. She sets out as many lamps as possible so it will seem the veil has disappeared. Mellie's house looks very lived in, even though it isn't. Mellie opens all the doors so I can see all the rooms. They are all the same, with a big bed and a mirror with a gold frame above the bed. The gold frame made me think of

Rose's mirror. But that was a miniature mirror since she could hold it in her hand. Towards the end, Rose used to spend hours looking in her little mirror. I wonder what she was looking at, since she could hardly see. Rose's mirror was one of the souvenirs that she broke on her last day. Mellie says nothing has been changed about the rooms. There are still dresses and shawls in the trunks. Mellie did not sell anything to the secondhand man. She has been living alone in this house for twelve years. She says she never met the owner, who died with no heirs. Mellie is the last manager of the boardinghouse. There were many other managers before her. The house is very old. There used to be women living in all the rooms. Mellie looked after them all. I asked her why the lodgers had all gone away when the house is so inviting. Mellie says the Charms neighborhood emptied out all of a sudden when the inland port closed. She didn't want to abandon the house, since she was the last manager. She asked me where I lived before I moved into Nem's house. I told her I had always lived at the Hermitage with Rose. Mellie says she knew Rose. She was a lodger in her house. Mellie showed me her room, room 3. There is a photo of a girl on the wall. Mellie says it's Rose. But the photo does not look like the one in the hallway of Nem's house. I asked Mellie if Rose lived in her house and in Nem's house. Mellie doesn't know what to say. Her memory is not all that good. She gets names and dates mixed up. I am her first visitor in twelve years. Nem never visits her. Mellie says he mistakes her for his old servant. She says her house is Rose's house. She is bored now that her house is empty. Before, the lodgers had many visitors. Things were always lively. Now Charms Way is nothing, no one ever comes this way. Mellie looks sad thinking about the old days.

Mellie invited me into her parlor. She has a parlor adjoining her room, since she is the manager. She gave me the best chair. She insisted I try some of her liqueurs. Her house used to be known for its liqueurs. All the lodgers had liqueurs, and offered them to their guests. Mellie says liqueurs improve with age, so they are even better now than before. She pours me a drop of each one so I can taste them all. I am not used to liqueurs, they make my head spin. Mellie is in no hurry to see me leave. Her hands shake. She spills liqueur over the side when she tries to pour it into the little glasses. She makes me think of Rose. Rose's hands also shook towards the end, when she held her little mirror in her hand. Mellie never stops repeating my name, which is also hers. Maybe she is repeating it to remind herself that her name is Mellie. She asked me to come and live in her house. She says Nem does not need company, he only needs someone to look after him and his house to replace his dead servant. I told Mellie that Rose wrote 7 Charms Street on the last page of my book of legends, she did not write Way, she wrote Street. Mellie says Charms Street is actually Charms Way. The street signs fell down and the city worker mixed them up when he put them back. The city worker doesn't know the

Charms neighborhood, he only knows the boulevard leading to the port. He always gets it wrong when he puts street signs back up. You think you are on a street when really you are on a way. I told Mellie I want to trust the street signs as they are now. Mellie seemed sad. To console her, I told her I would come and visit her often. She told me to come see her every Thursday. Thursday was her favorite day in the old days to receive visitors. She has already forgotten that she asked me to come and live in her house. She is thinking about next Thursday and the way Thursdays used to be. I asked her where Storks Street is. Storks Street is very close, at the end of Charms Way. Mellie took a keyring from her pocket, and she gave me a key. She says the key opens her house and Nem's house. It is the same lock. It's the key to Rose's house.

Storks Street is a street with only one house. I understand why the photographer lives at number 1 since that is the only number. He lives in a big stone house. This is the first stone house I have seen in Oât. It's solidly built, there is no sign of deterioration anywhere. The photographer wears a black suit, undoubtedly a photographer's suit. He is old, but not nearly as old as Nem and Mellie. His house is at an intersection. He says it is in the very center of the Charms neighborhood. But Storks Street is not part of the Charms neighborhood, it's separate. I told the photographer right away that Miss Martha sent me to be photographed. He showed me into a very large room. There are no rooms

this big at Nem's or Mellie's. It's an exhibition room with cameras set up everywhere on tall stools. This really is a
32 photographer's house. He told me right away that none of these cameras work. They are very old, very rare cameras from his private collection. All the cameras come from the continent. The secondhand man bought them for him on his trips to the continent. His collection is not complete yet. The photographer hopes it will rival the Museum on the continent soon. He thinks Oât needs a museum. When his collection is complete, he will open the museum of Oât at 1 Storks Street. He wants Miss Martha to be the curator. He thinks the municipal offices at the port are not the right place for her. He built up his collection with Miss Martha in mind, so he could found the museum and she could be the curator. He is attached to Miss Martha. He says he was an architect before he became a photographer. He never did anything with his first profession because he says it is an impracticable profession. Now he thinks photography is also impracticable. That's why he is dedicating himself to completing his collection for the future museum of Oât. He describes the characteristics of each camera as if I were a visitor to his museum. To me, all the cameras look the same despite their characteristics.

Fortunately, the photographer remembered all of a sudden that I had come to be photographed. He told me this would be his last photo for the municipal offices. He is taking my picture to please Miss Martha. He says Miss

Martha grew up in the Charms neighborhood. She was always drawn to the photographer's house. He says Miss Martha has not turned out like he hoped. He hardly rec- ognizes her anymore since she started working in the municipal offices at the port. He says it is because of her bad choice of friends. He looks sad when he thinks of what Miss Martha has become. It is as if he had forgotten about the future of his museum. He took a little camera out of a cabinet, a brand-new camera that has nothing in common with the old cameras in his collection. It's the latest-model polaroid, the most advanced one ever. It takes color snapshots of excellent quality. The photographer tried to give it to Miss Martha, but she wanted nothing to do with it. He sat me down on a stool by the window. I heard a click from the polaroid. A few minutes later, I had my photograph. I looked at myself for a long time. It is not at all the same as looking at myself in the mirror. On the back of the photo, I wrote: *Mellie aged twelve, photographed by the photographer of Oât at 1 Storks Street.* Being photographed for the first time is a real occasion for me. The photographer told me it was useless to write on the back of the photo since Miss Martha would glue it onto my identity card and I would never be able to reread what I had written. It doesn't matter, I still needed to write on the back of my first photograph. I wrote in small letters as carefully as I could, I wrote in the old alphabet. Soon I hope I will know how to write in the new alphabet too.

I had already left when the photographer called me

back. It was to give me his polaroid. He doesn't want any more polaroids in his house. He asked me to tell Miss Martha that even in exceptional cases, he would take no more photographs for the municipal offices. He did not want me to thank him for the polaroid. He showed me how it works. There is a roll of film with twelve photos. Now there are eleven left. I would never have thought I would own a polaroid and be able to take color snapshots. I put the polaroid in my bag. From now on, I will always go out with my bag because I always want to have my polaroid with me in case there is a photo I want to take. The photographer doesn't realize what a gift he is giving me. The polaroid is better than his whole collection of old cameras for the future museum of Oât.

The key Mellie gave me really does open the door of Nem's house. Nem is not at his writing desk. He is sitting on his balcony and looking at the flowering tree. The first flowers have just fallen because of the wind that came up all of a sudden. There is a little pink carpet just at the foot of the tree. The wind comes into the room, the smell from the lagoon is stronger. It is undoubtedly going to rain.

I showed my photo to Nem right away. He says it is not a good likeness. He will say anything at all. A photo is always a good likeness. It's just that he is not used to color photos. The photo hanging up in his hallway is in black and white. He says that one is a good likeness. How can he know that? I can't trust what he says. His shelf is empty.

He put the big books back in the crate. The big notebooks are gone from the writing desk. Something has happened.

Nem took his time before he told me about the sec- ondhand man's visit. When the secondhand man came to buy the sign, Nem showed him up to his room. Nem said he suddenly wondered what the secondhand man would think of his big books, which he had never before shown to anyone. The secondhand man recognized them right away. They were old books from the continent, and the old alphabet that Nem deciphered so badly is the old alphabet of the continent. Nem has never been to the continent, so he could not know the old alphabet of the continent. The secondhand man was interested in Nem's translations. He says his translations of the old books from the continent into the old alphabet of Oât are the only ones that exist and that they are good translations. He offered to buy them from Nem and sell them to the Library on the continent. Nem agreed to sell them so he could be rid of them. But he still thinks they are bad translations, and that he deciphered the alphabet incorrectly. He says the secondhand man knows nothing about the old alphabet and that his judgment is meaningless. He says it is because he comes from Oât that he could not decipher the old alphabet of the continent. He says he should have been born on the continent and not in Oât. He says his whole life is a mistake, even his birth was a mistake. His writing desk is empty now that he has sold his big notebooks to the secondhand man. Nem says he lived closed up in the library studying the old alphabet of Oât when it was the old alphabet of the continent that he should have been studying. He doesn't know what he is doing anymore in Rose's house. He says he has always been no one, even when he was the librarian of Oât he was no one.

Before he went to bed, Nem told me I had come too late. He is confusing me with the girl whose photograph is in the hall. He takes me for Rose, even though I tell him my name is Mellie and not Rose. I looked at my photo again. It looks nothing like the one in the hallway. I don't have a photo of Rose. She must not have liked photos, otherwise she would have given me one. I get Rose a little mixed up with Mellie. It's a good thing I am not living in Mellie's house. In the end I would think Mellie is Rose. But I want Rose to be Rose. Names get mixed up easily if you aren't careful. That must be what is happening to Nem, who thinks I am Rose when really my name is Mellie. I never knew Rose's last name. When I tried to go to the office of records and notify them of Rose's death like Miss Martha said, I could only give her first name. Miss Martha would not have thought that was enough. Fortunately, the attendant was on the telephone. She didn't hear me when I notified her of Rose's death because she had the receiver to her ear. She thought I was saying goodbye, she did not think I was notifying her of a death. So she didn't record Rose's death in her register. Miss Martha would be angry if

she knew that. But I would rather Rose had no death certificate on file in the municipal offices of Oât. That does
not mean she isn't dead.

§6

Miss Martha thought my photo was a very good likeness.
She glued it to my temporary identity card. She put the
stamp of the municipal offices on the photo, and then she
signed it. There we are, I am now in possession of my
permanent identity card. It does not take much to go from
a temporary identity card to a permanent identity card. I
told Miss Martha that the photographer had asked me to
tell her he would never take any more photographs for the
municipal offices. I also told her that he gave me the polaroid. Miss Martha said he did the right thing, I was the
right age for a polaroid. She doesn't like me to talk about
the photographer. All the same, I asked her if it would
please her to become the curator of the future museum of
Oât. She said there will never be a museum in Oât. The
people here are not interested in cameras, and the travelers
who stop off in Oât have all been to the Museum on the
continent which is beyond comparison with the museum
the photographer wants to open. Miss Martha says photography was a youthful mistake of hers.

There is no question of Miss Martha giving up her position in the municipal offices. She has worked her way up.
She is not only an employee of the reception center, even
though she has kept that title. Now she is the deputy

mayor. And since the mayor has gone to live on the continent, she is in charge. Being deputy mayor in the mayor's
absence is almost the same as being mayor. Miss Martha hopes to take his place in the next election. The mayor will not run, since he never wants to come back to Oât. Miss Martha thinks she has a good chance of being elected. She proved her competence by carrying out the functions of deputy mayor. She wants to see the port of Oât develop. It's a stroke of luck that she has taken an interest in me, considering the high rank she occupies in the municipal offices.

Nem lives closed up in his room. He says that now he wants to forget about time so he can forget about the old alphabet of the continent. He wants to forget about the old alphabet of the continent. He says that if he manages to forget about time he might get his memory back. Ever since it started to rain, it has been raining almost constantly. The vacant land is half flooded. I am learning the new alphabet thanks to the pamphlets Miss Martha gave me. It is easy to learn. I work from morning to evening in my room. I am making good progress. Miss Martha corrects my exercises. There are no mistakes. Miss Martha thinks I am a good student and that I have abilities. I can already read the posters in the municipal offices. All the city ordinances are posted in the hallway of the municipal offices. Miss Martha wants me to put my name down as an unaffiliated candidate for the certificate. She says it is always good to have the certificate, especially when you don't have the diploma. When Miss Martha was young, you could get your diploma as an unaffiliated candidate, but now it is impossible. All the girls from Oât who had abilities left for the continent to get their diplomas, and they never came back. Miss Martha gave me more pamphlets to complete my study of the new alphabet and to prepare me for the certificate. I like to study alone in my room. It rains every day. The noise doesn't bother me. Nem never makes any noise. The material for the certificate is simple. Rose taught me a great deal. She knew far more than is necessary for the certificate. Without my knowing it, she gave me a taste for study.

I will not be a translator since there will never be a library in the municipal offices like Miss Martha wanted. The mayor gave the order to send all the old books from the former library of Oât to the Library on the continent. The more I learn the new alphabet, the more I think I would have run into difficulties as I translated. It would be better for me to get my certificate and to apply for the position of secretary to the mayor, which is open. Miss Martha lives alone in the staff lodgings on the top floor of the municipal offices. She devotes all her time to the municipal offices, except Sundays. Time is passing quickly as I finish learning the new alphabet and study for the certificate. Miss Martha is pleased with me. She told me that I could enjoy my Sunday off since I had worked so well. She said she had a surprise for me.

I went to meet Miss Martha at four o'clock. This is my first Sunday with Miss Martha. She decided to take me to the tea dance at the Continental. She says the Continental is the most fashionable bar of the port, with the best clientele. I was surprised to see Miss Martha in her Sunday clothes. I have never seen her so elegant. She always dresses severely at the municipal offices. She was wearing a sheath dress made of black satin with a little white fur collar and a matching toque. She was also wearing pumps that make her seem more willowy, and she has a little lizardskin purse that matches her pumps. It's a good thing I have my polaroid in my bag. I took my first photo in front of the Continental. On the back of the photograph, I wrote: *Miss Martha in her black satin sheath dress and her white fur collar with matching toque, in front of the Continental, the day of my first tea dance.* It really is a good photo. The sun came out just as I was taking the photo. You can see the Continental's sign behind Miss Martha. I wrote in the old alphabet, as small as possible. But now that I also know the new alphabet, I can choose between the two alphabets. Miss Martha thought it was childish of me to write on the back of the photo. I told her that I am not a child anymore since I have had my first period and I am not a virgin. She smiled, she said that still doesn't mean I am not a child.

We sat as close to the dance floor as possible, so we would have the best view. Miss Martha ordered two hot chocolates and two éclairs. Her eyes are shining. She danced every dance. She often changes partners. I was the one who drank the two hot chocolates and ate the two éclairs. I am very thirsty and very hungry. I asked Miss Martha if she often came to the tea dances at the Continental. She comes every Sunday. She is a regular. Between the dances, she often goes downstairs to the restroom. I saw her going down the stairs. Above the stairs at the far end of the dance floor, there is a sign that says: Restrooms, and an arrow pointing down. Now that I know the new alphabet, I can read all the signs. I don't dare follow Miss Martha, even though I really want to go down to the restroom also. I don't want her to think I am too curious and that I am following her everywhere. It was very nice of her to bring me to the tea dance. I would never have come alone since minors must be accompanied by an adult. I don't want to be a nuisance to Miss Martha. She must have habits of her own since she comes here every Sunday.

I said no when I was asked to dance. For now, I would rather watch and study the dance steps. It doesn't look hard, all you have to do is follow the rhythm like Miss Martha. She dances very well by following the rhythm. Miss Martha said I was lucky the jukebox had just been delivered. Until now, there was only a record player for the tea dances at the Continental. Miss Martha says there is no comparison between the music of the jukebox and the music of the record player. You can't see the ocean from the Continental because of the thick curtains on the windows. The light is filtered. You would never think it was afternoon. I noticed that when Miss Martha goes down to the restroom there is always a gentleman following her.

Leaving the Continental, we walked along the boulevard of the port. We passed by the Dance Palace. I asked Miss Martha if there were also tea dances on Sunday afternoons at the Dance Palace. Miss Martha said yes, but that it was not well frequented. And yet there seems to be a great deal of atmosphere at the Dance Palace with an orchestra instead of a jukebox, and the terrace overlooking the ocean is filled with people. Miss Martha repeated that the Continental is more exclusive than the Dance Palace. I don't want to contradict her. She really has shown me a great deal of kindness. The Continental is her weakness. She admitted, as if she was telling me something in confidence that she had never told anyone before, that she also went there in the evening after midnight. It's reserved for club members then. After midnight, the Continental is a private club. Miss Martha took a membership card from her lizardskin purse. They only give the card to adults. So I will not go to the Continental after midnight with Miss Martha. There is undoubtedly a big difference between afternoons and after-midnights at the Continental. Miss Martha seems to prefer the after-midnights. It must be when she has been to the Continental after midnight that in the morning she looks drawn and suddenly older than she is.

For my visit to the tea dance, Miss Martha gave me a red velvet dress with a matching bolero. It's a dress that follows the shape of the body and shows the body to its best advantage. Miss Martha says it was her first fancy outfit as a young girl. She says she is glad that I am wearing it in my turn, because she was the same size I am when she was my age. That is not completely true. The dress is a little tight on me. Miss Martha says she was developed at the same age as me. But I must be more developed than she was. She gave me a pair of red slippers that match my dress. I would have preferred pumps so I would look taller. This is the first time I have been dressed all in red.

All week long I looked forward to Sunday. On Sunday, I went to meet Miss Martha exactly at four o'clock. She was wearing her black satin sheath dress and I was wearing my red velvet dress with the bolero. We sat down at the same table just at the edge of the dance floor. That table is especially reserved for Miss Martha. This time, I didn't miss a single dance. I danced with Pim. Pim is a sailor. Specifically, he said he was an officer candidate. Every week, he makes a round trip on a big ship between Oât and the continent. On Sundays, the ship always docks at Oât because the officers enjoy the tea dances at the Continental. Pim is a good dancer. He knows how to lead. He told me I dance well for my first time. After several dances, there was a break. Pim suggested we go down to the restroom. He followed me into the ladies' room. I didn't say anything, he seems to know his way around. The first stall is occupied, I went into the second one. Pim followed me.

He slid the lock on the door. Now both stalls are occupied. I did everything like Pim wanted me to. He is more used

to the ladies' room than I am. He says the Continental's ladies' rooms are well-known and it is because of the restrooms that the Continental is so busy on Sunday afternoons. Even though Pim is only an officer candidate, he is experienced. He had me kneel on the rim of the toilet bowl. He took off my underwear, but he wanted me to keep on my dress and my slippers. He only hitched up my dress. He didn't take the time to caress me. He wanted everything right away. He said we must not miss the next dance. But the break lasts long enough. This is the first time from behind. Pim bit my neck and dug his nails into my stomach. I squeezed the waterpipe very hard. I let out a little cry. Pim put his hands over my mouth. You must not cry out in the restrooms of the Continental, it isn't done. When we had finished with our pleasure, Pim told me I had a lovely bottom. Now I am even more of a real girl, now that Pim took me from behind while I was kneeling on the rim. I like to go down to the ladies' room with Pim. We went back up to the dance floor as soon as we heard the music from the jukebox. But we came back down to the restrooms two more times. Each time, Pim made me kneel on the rim of the bowl.

After Miss Martha and I left the Continental, we walked along the boulevard of the port like last Sunday. I talked about Pim. I also told her we went down to the restrooms and what we did in the stall. Miss Martha smiled, she said I was the right age for that. She squeezed my arm very hard. I didn't ask her what she did when she goes down to the restrooms with one of the dancers. If she wanted to tell me, she would. At her age, she undoubtedly does not do the same things as me.

I would miss it if I couldn't go to the Sunday tea dances anymore. Pim is as impatient as I am for next Sunday. What would I do if I didn't go to the Continental on Sundays? Oât is even more lifeless on Sundays than during the week. And I can't count on Nem to keep me company. He goes out all day without telling me where he is going. He never comes back until the end of the afternoon, to rest in his courtyard as usual. He watches the flowers falling from the tree one after another. He never hooks up his hearing device anymore. He says it's broken. So it is impossible to have a conversation with him. At his age, it is not good to go outside where everything is damp from the rains. He goes outside even when it is raining. Miss Martha wants what is best for me. She has me do little jobs around the office while I am waiting to get my certificate. The mayor's office pays me a small stipend. That gives me some pocket money. The last flowers fell off the tree. The courtyard is all pink. I took a picture of Nem sitting on his low chair in the courtyard. But Nem deliberately moved when he saw that I was taking his picture. He was cut off, you can only see half of Nem. The photo is all pink because of the flowers that had fallen from the tree and that cover the courtyard. On the back of the photo, I wrote: *7 Charms Street, the courtyard covered with pink flowers from the tree and Nem cut off because he moved while I was taking his picture.* You can't recognize Nem in the photo.

Now that Nem is always out, I go out too. I have nothing more to study, I have studied all the pamphlets. I always go in the direction of the lagoon. The closer you get to the lagoon, the more deserted it becomes and the more the houses are run down. Markers Street runs right along the lagoon. The houses were built only on one side. On the other side must have been the piers of the port which the lagoon covered little by little. The houses on Markers Street are in ruins, except one. Its facade is still in good condition, undoubtedly because it was built of stone. But the facade is deceptive. The inside is dilapidated. The staircase to the second floor is still there. One part of the second floor has collapsed, but there is still one bedroom intact with all its furniture. The armoire is full of clothes. There are wedding clothes in it. I removed them to air them out. I found two mannequins at the back of the closet. They are seamstress's mannequins. Maybe this was a seamstress's house. I dressed the mannequins in the wedding clothes. The clothes are just their size. There is a bride and a groom. All that is missing is the bride's veil and the groom's hat. I laid the newlyweds down on the bed. I take a rest in the bedroom before leaving. I look at the lagoon from the window. The water looks dirty. It's stagnant water, you can smell it. In the middle of the lagoon there is a big rusty ship slowly sinking into the water. It must be the wreck of a ship that was imprisoned in the lagoon when the channel filled up with sand. I noticed a little boat moving in the direction of the big ship. I thought I saw Nem. So when he goes out, it is so he can go boating on the lagoon. That is not wise at his age. He still wants to forget about time. Maybe he can forget about it on the lagoon. Far away, I see the beginning of the forest. In clear weather, I can also see the mountains where the Hermitage is. But I never forget that I am in Oât. Mellie 3175 is a funny name to say who I am.

§7

I put my photos between the pages of my book of legends. It's a little like a picture book. There is the photo of Miss Martha and the photo of Nem, there is also the photo glued on my identity card. The book is prominently displayed on my bookshelf. I had the idea of putting up the sign from the Hermitage above the door to my room. I put it up on the inside so it is not visible from the hallway and so that I can see it from my bed. When I look at the door to my room, it is as if I was looking at the door to the Hermitage.

The secondhand man is the only person who lives on Wardens Square. The square is not as lovely as Nem claims it is. The facades of the old administrative buildings are made of molded plaster, but the plaster is discolored and cracked everywhere, and there are black streaks because of the broken gutters. The old administrative buildings of Oât are not very impressive, and the municipality of the port no longer maintains them now that they are closed. There is only one house of any distinction on Wardens Square, and that is the former town hall. Now it is the secondhand man's house. The former town hall was much more impressive than the new one, which is part of the Customs office. The secondhand man uses the old administrative buildings as warehouses. The secondhand man has business dealings with the continent. He is having a big house built on the continent where he will spend the rest of his days. He says that soon there will be nothing more to buy in Oât.

The secondhand man often invites me to his house. I know why he is being so nice to me. Nem was right, the secondhand man wants to buy the Hermitage sign from me. He is hoping to exchange it for some old jewelry that he keeps in a case and that he shows me every time I come to see him. He says it's valuable jewelry of unknown origin. He says it would be a good deal to trade the sign for the case. Each time I come, he opens the case and I admire the jewelry. The case tempts me, otherwise I would not come so often to see the secondhand man and all the clutter in his house. The jewelry has blue stones. There are several different kinds of jewelry. The secondhand man wanted me to try them on. This is the first time I have tried on jewelry. I didn't want to look at myself in the mirror with the jewelry on for fear that I might never be able to take it off. The secondhand man tries to tempt me every way he knows how. He says that with the jewels I will have everything I want. But I do not want to sell my sign, so I will not let myself be tempted.

Now I never try on the jewelry when I go to see the secondhand man. I only admire it in its case. The stones in the jewelry are blue like the ocean and like Yem's eyes. I have not seem Yem since I met him the first day by his fishing boat. And yet I have gone back many times to sit on the dock. The Queen of the Fairies was never docked there. A fisherman told me Yem had gone with his skipper on a long voyage to Ot. Ot is an island very far from Oât. Yem had not told me about the voyage. I would rather not come back anymore to sit on the dock so I won't have to think about the Queen of the Fairies or about Yem.

I never forget to visit Mellie on Thursdays. Mellie wants to meet Miss Martha, since I have told her so much about her. But Miss Martha refuses all Mellie's invitations. Even though she grew up in the Charms neighborhood, she never wants to go back there. She even asked me what I saw in Mellie. I don't ask her what she sees in the Continental after midnight. Between Miss Martha and me, there is one point of disagreement, and that is the Charms neighborhood. Fortunately we share a taste for the tea dances at the Continental.

Mellie finally gave up hoping for a visit from Miss Martha. She will make do with my visits. In my honor, she put her parlor back the way it used to be when she had so many visitors. She took the slipcovers off the furniture. She tried to wind the clock. But the clock has stopped working, the mechanism is broken. And there is not a single clockmaker left in Oât. Mellie bought back her phonograph and her records from the secondhand man. She had sold them to him for almost nothing. She was angry because she had to pay more for them than she sold them for. But the secondhand man threw in a new needle for her phonograph. Mellie is glad that her records don't sound so scratchy anymore. In the end she does not regret having bought back her phonograph. She sold it because it was too sad to listen to the phonograph all alone. Now she is beginning to find her taste for music again. She says that with me she can hear all the songs of her life again. She always offers me the same liqueurs with slightly stale cookies specially made for dipping in the liqueurs. The liqueurs no longer make my head spin. The alcohol must be evaporating. Mellie never closes the decanters anymore. She never drinks anything, she says she is too old for liqueurs. Her pleasure comes from watching me eat and drink. She says I look like she did at my age. Mellie also turned her big painting around. She had turned it to the wall. It's a portrait of a girl. The colors are a little faded, but the portrait is well drawn. There is no signature on the painting. Mellie says it is a portrait of Rose. And yet the girl in the portrait looks nothing like the photo of Rose in room 3. Mellie says it was thanks to Rose that her house on

Charms Way had such a good reputation in the old days. The parlor is not the same now that the painting has been turned around.

I am attached to Mellie. Her hands tremble a little more every week. Each time, I talk to her about Rose. Now Mellie tells me that all the lodgers who lived in room 3 were named Rose. So which Rose do I want her to tell me about? Mellie gets them all confused. To console me for her inability to talk to me about Rose like I want, she opened the trunk in room 3. It's a trunk full of dresses. Mellie says they are all Rose's dresses. She chose one and gave it to me. It's a white muslin dress. Mellie gave me the pumps that go with it, and a shawl to put over the dress, which is very low-cut. The skirt is very full with all its little gathers. The seamstress who made this dress had to have a great deal of patience and skill to sew all those little gathers. It is sewn so carefully that the seams are invisible. I kissed Mellie for having given me such a lovely gift. Thanks to Mellie, now I have a second dress to wear to the tea dances at the Continental.

Miss Martha thought I looked old-fashioned in my white muslin dress. She said I was too young for it. It is just my size and it's comfortable to wear. I told Miss Martha that muslin is more flattering than velvet and that white goes better with my skin than red. I am standing up to Miss Martha. She is unhappy that I have changed dresses and that I prefer the white muslin dress to the red velvet dress.

I am not going to wear the same dress forever just to please Miss Martha.

Pim is very pleased with my new dress. He says it gives me a unique style and that I don't look like anyone else. Muslin is easier to hitch up than velvet, especially since my velvet dress is a little tight and you always have to be careful not to tear it at the seams. With my muslin dress, there is no danger. I get along well with Pim. We spend more time in the ladies' room than on the dance floor. Now even between the breaks we sometimes go down to the restrooms. Both stalls are always free between the breaks. You can choose the one you want. But there is no difference between the two stalls in the ladies' room at the Continental.

Pim is sad. He is going to change ships, and he will never come back to Oât. He would like to refuse, but he can't. He has to prove himself as an officer candidate. He is leaving for a trip around the world as a way of proving himself. Our last Sunday was our best Sunday, even though Pim was sad. After the tea dance, I walked Pim back to his ship. This is the first time I have gone with him instead of taking a walk along the boulevard of the port with Miss Martha. Next Sunday, Pim will be far from Oât. I would have liked to go on board Pim's ship to say goodbye to him on the deck. But the ship is forbidden to women and girls. It's a big ship. Pim looked at me for a long time from the deck and I looked at him from the pier. My legs hurt from standing so long without moving and looking at him for as long as he looked at me. But I didn't want to leave as long as he was on the deck. He would have been even more sad if I had left. We stayed there looking at each other, him on the deck and me on the pier, until night came. Then we no longer saw each other.

I will miss Pim, but I am not really sad. Miss Martha says none of the dancers at the Continental are irreplaceable. She may be right. And then the restrooms were small and uncomfortable. It gave me cramps always to be kneeling on the edge of the bowl without ever being able to change positions. If you stayed that way a little too long, as we did more and more these past few Sundays, there would be knocks on the door. You had to come out right away so as not to annoy the others impatiently waiting their turn. Two stalls is not enough. Furthermore, the bowl was cracked. I was always afraid it would break if I moved too much. The tank was beginning to leak. I had drops of water falling on my neck and rolling down my back, which made my white muslin dress wet. Pim was not sensitive to all these practical details. He always thought the ladies' room at the Continental was the best thing there is. But I was more and more aware of those details, which were about to ruin the pleasure I felt at being with Pim. In my opinion the restrooms at the Continental are overrated.

Miss Martha did not go down to the restrooms these last few Sundays. She even turned down invitations to dance sometimes. When I told her Pim would never be back and that I did not want to go to the tea dances without Pim, she seemed relieved. She had made it her job to accompany me since I was a minor. But now she would rather use her Sundays to rest and to catch up on her sleep. Little by little, the after-midnights at the Continental have made her lose her taste for the afternoons. I can understand that, because I also lost my taste for the afternoons even though I don't know anything about the after-midnights. All it took to make me stop wanting to go to the tea dances at the Continental was for Pim to go off on his trip around the world.

I am worried about Mellie. She is going downhill very quickly all of a sudden. She trembles more and more. She leaves everything in a mess in her parlor. She never even washes out the little liqueur glasses anymore. She broke the decanters. It smells like liqueur all over her house. Her cataract is becoming worse. The veil in front of her eyes no longer disappears when she stands near a lamp. The lamps are on for no reason. Mellie is too weak to look after Nem. I am the one who looks after Nem and his house in Mellie's place. I would like to come and live in Mellie's house, but I can't abandon Nem, who is going downhill as fast as Mellie. Ever since Mellie stopped looking after him, he thinks she is dead. His mind is going. He confuses Mellie with his dead servant. He mourns the death of his servant. He asked the secondhand man to come and empty out his room. The secondhand man took away the crate full of big books. Nem says his memory is coming back and that he is forgetting about time. His boat rides on the lagoon are not very good for him. He never stops coughing. It keeps me from sleeping. Nem says he should have looked for Rose instead of coming and living in the house she had left. It is as if he didn't know who I am. He no longer takes me for Rose, but now he doesn't take me for anyone. He has forgotten my name. Mellie is only the name of the servant whose death he is mourning. He says it might not be too late to look for Rose.

The attendant at the office of records has gone to live on the continent. I have replaced her in the little glassed-in office. Until I get my certificate, I will only be an assistant. The day of the exam is approaching. I am ready. I have nothing but deaths to record in the office of records. It's always very old people dying. There are no births or marriages. Miss Martha is hoping things will turn around soon. The elections are approaching. Miss Martha had big posters put up all along the boulevard. She sent promotional packages to the voters. As expected, the mayor is not running. Miss Martha is certain to be elected because she is the only candidate. She has taken on an air of importance. She is always hurrying somewhere when I see her. The repopulation of Oât is the main thrust of her electoral campaign. She says once she becomes mayor she will have full powers and she will be able to carry out all her projects. She is a woman of action. She accuses the mayor. When he left to live on the continent, he was set-

56 ting a bad example. He had a certain influence over the people of Oât. All the forward-looking citizens wanted to follow his lead. Miss Martha would like to think the de-population of Oât is not irreversible. Mellie says it is irre-versible. Even though the port was built right on the ocean, its future is in danger. Mellie says it is because of a lack of resources, and that there is nothing to be done about a lack of resources.

I go to see Mellie every day, not only on Thursday any-more. Mellie has just informed me that the time has come for her to leave Charms Way. She gave me the big painting that was hanging in her parlor. She wanted me to wrap it up carefully because she says it's a very fragile painting. I took it to my room, but my room is too small for such a big painting. So I left it wrapped up, and I leaned it against the wall. I am very touched that Mellie gave me her painting. It was her prized possession. She called the secondhand man, and she told him he could empty out the house now. The secondhand man has been waiting a long time for this day. Mellie has decided to spend her last days in the hospital. She says the hospital has a very good reputation. It was endowed by the continent for the peo-ple of Oât. Mellie says she will have a view of the ocean for the first time. She has enough to pay for the hospital with the money the secondhand man gave her for all the things he took away. I was sad to see Mellie leaving for the hospital and the secondhand man emptying out her house. Mellie is not sad to be going. She says she will have company in the hospital. She asked to be in the main ward and not in a private room.

I have never taken a photo of Mellie. Every time I went to see her, I had my bag with my polaroid in it, and every time I forgot to photograph her. At the hospital, they told me I would have to wait to visit Mellie until she became accustomed to her new life. So I photographed the hospital, on the side that faces the ocean, where all the bay windows are. I put an X on the photo. The X marks the bay window that Mellie's bed is in front of. The nurse who looks after her and who tells me how she is doing told me which bay window it was. On the back of the photo, I wrote: *The hospital where Mellie wanted to spend her last days lying on her bed in front of the bay window overlooking the ocean.* It doesn't look like a hospital, you would think it was a photo of a villa by the sea.

As I was leaving the hospital, I saw the word clinic written on a door on the ground floor. Suddenly I remembered the medical examination. I had completely forgotten to go. They found me to be in good health. My period started just in time for the medical examination. They gave me a pamphlet with information about reproduction and the menstrual cycle. The pamphlet isn't signed. It was not written by Miss Martha, it isn't written in her style at all.

I passed the test for the certificate with a rating of very good. Apparently I am even the first candidate ever to get a perfect score. Miss Martha was elected mayor. She is in the mayor's office, which was closed until now. I hardly recognize her now that I have stopped going to the Continental with her. She puts on airs now that she is the mayor. She appointed me clerk of the office of records and secretary to the mayor. I fulfill both functions. They are cutting down on personnel. Before I can be permanently appointed, I will be on probation. I have to prove myself. I am not yet old enough for a permanent appointment. I am earning a real salary now that I have my certificate.

§8

The tree in Nem's courtyard has bloomed again. Today is my birthday. I am thirteen years old. It has been a year since Rose died and I left the Hermitage. Nem doesn't know that today is my birthday, he doesn't know that I am thirteen. He doesn't know anything about me. He sits on his balcony so he can see the pink flowers on the tree, which are just in front of him when he is on the balcony. He is astonished that the tree has bloomed again. He thought the tree would never bloom again because it is very old.

Mellie is quite used to the hospital. I go to see her every Thursday now. She expects my visits, but she never recognizes me anymore. She calls me Rose. She is in a room with other very old women like her. Her bed faces the ocean. Mellie is spending the end of her life looking at the ocean. She says she can still see well enough, but that the ocean gets a little less blue every day. She is not suffer- ing. She must hardly be able to feel her body anymore, she is so weak. Her long white hair is undone. She never puts on her bonnet anymore. When I go to see her, I spend a long time combing her hair. That's what she likes best. I don't like the hospital. Everything there is blue and white. Mellie wears a blue nightgown and her sheets are an immaculate white.

Miss Martha has announced many ordinances since she was elected mayor. But her ordinances have no effect. Oât is still losing its population. Mellie is right to say it is irreversible. The municipal offices are almost always deserted. Miss Martha is very hurt by her failure. She says mayor is a meaningless title. She is becoming closer to me again. Important matters are decided on the continent. It is as if Oât had no mayor at all. Miss Martha is always on the outside. She has no say in anything. In the afternoon, she asks me to her lodgings for tea. She needs to talk. She says I look much older than my age and that I have matured a great deal in the past year. She confides in me. She says she is disenchanted with everything, not just the municipal offices. The after-midnights at the Continental are also a failure. Miss Martha devoted herself to them completely, but she did not get what she wanted from them. The club is not what it used to be. It's losing all its members to a new club on the continent: the Blue Island. It just opened recently, but it has already made a name for itself. Miss Martha dreams of the Blue Island. She says nothing will come of the Continental, which is letting itself be beaten out by the Dance Palace. The triumph of the Dance Palace over the Continental torments Miss Martha.

For the first time, Miss Martha is tempted by the continent. She says she can start over at the Blue Island. She will not be responsible for the municipal offices of Oât if she goes and lives on the continent. Now she knows it is impossible to be the mayor of Oât because Oât is not governable. She says the mayor was right to leave. She has realized that too late. She blames herself for her lack of judgment and experience. She says growing up in the Charms neighborhood gave her a false impression of Oât. She is overcome by all the things she is discovering at once. They have offered her a job as head of the Blue Island. She would never have dared hope to be able to devote herself to just one task. She says she doesn't want to go on living a double life, split between the municipal offices of Oât and the Continental. Double lives always end badly. It will not be long before the Continental closes. The competition of the Dance Palace was too much for it. For Miss Martha, that's an additional reason to leave, even if she says she has not yet made a decision.

The Dance Palace is not forbidden to minors, and even unaccompanied minors are allowed in to the Sunday afternoon tea dances. Miss Martha hid that from me so that I would always go with her to the Continental. I am bored on Sundays ever since Pim left. There is a big crowd on Sunday afternoons on the terrace of the Dance Palace. Why shouldn't I go to the tea dances at Dance Palace too? Spending all week at the municipal offices and Sundays at Nem's house is no way to live. Nem is never there since the secondhand man emptied out his room. He is always in his boat on the lagoon. He circles around the big rusty ship in his boat. The hull has almost completely disappeared into the lagoon. The tree in the courtyard lost all its flowers in just one day. It was a day of high winds and rain. The flowers withered as soon as they fell.

Today is Sunday and I am going to the Dance Palace for the first time. Too bad if Miss Martha finds out and becomes angry. She thinks about nothing but the Blue Island anyway. I put on my red velvet dress with the bolero like the first time I went to the Continental with Miss Martha. My red dress brought me luck once, maybe it will bring me luck twice. At the Dance Palace, the lady in the cloak room showed me into a little parlor. It looks onto the terrace, but it's separated from it by a pane of glass. On the other side of the glass the dancers come and go, undoubtedly to look at me since I am new to the Dance Palace. I am sitting on a chair. I am very visible in my red velvet dress. I feel a little lost. There is a stairway going up. The one in the Continental went down. The orchestra plays very loudly. There are a lot of people going up the stairs. I don't see any kind of a sign at the bottom of the stairs. Nothing is indicated, you have to know the way.

I was still sitting on the chair in the little parlor when suddenly I saw the truck driver come in. He saw me at the same time I saw him. He seemed surprised and unhappy to run into me there. He asked me what I was doing at the Dance Palace, as if it were not a place for me. I told him right away that this was my first Sunday at the Dance Palace. Before this, I always used to go to the Continental with Miss Martha. I also told the driver that I had not left the little parlor since I had come into the Dance Palace, I haven't been out on the terrace, I haven't even climbed the stairs. The driver looked at me more kindly. He doesn't seem angry anymore. He led me towards the exit.

His yellow truck, as well-polished as ever, is parked on the boulevard in front of the Dance Palace. The driver told me to get in. He is taking me for a drive. We drove up the boulevard, we followed a road that runs between the ocean and the lagoon. We crossed over the channel. I can see why the channel is unnavigable, with all those sand bars. After the channel, we drove through the dunes. The driver stopped his truck at the foot of a dune facing the ocean, at the beginning of a beach. He pushed the button on the seat, which opened up gently until it was a bunk. That brought back memories. The driver said I had changed, I look like a real girl now. He says he is happy to see me again. I am happy too, to be back on the bunk in the truck. You can still see the blood stain, but it's much lighter, the driver must have scrubbed it for a long time. More quickly than the first time, the driver took off my dress, my bolero, and my underwear. I am having my period again. That doesn't seem to bother the truck driver. He caresses me everywhere, like the first time. The sun comes in the window of the cab. The first time it was night and there was only the dome light. That changes everything. The driver remembered that he had me as a virgin. He says I am much more pleasing to him now. I told him everything that happened with Pim in the restrooms of the Continental. I do not want to hide anything from the truck driver. It seemed to please him that I told him how everything happened in the stall with Pim. He stopped caressing me, and he took me with just one very hard thrust. He says the bunk in the truck is more comfortable than the restrooms of the Continental. I agreed. He says I am made for the bunk of his truck. I didn't answer. He made me promise never to go back to the Dance Palace. He says the Dance Palace is not for me. I understood that he was very set on my promising that. So I promised. I don't want to ruin this Sunday afternoon by the ocean with the truck driver. I don't know what could be so terrible about the Dance Palace that Miss Martha and now the truck driver don't want me to go and dance there.

We got out of the cab. The beach is covered with seagulls. The driver told me this was called Seagull Beach. That's a good name for it. It is Oât's only beach. You can't see the end of it. I would like to walk along the beach with the truck driver for a long time without saying anything. But he wants to talk. He is not responsive to Seagull Beach like I am. He says tomorrow he will be leaving for the continent for good. This is his last day in Oât. He closed his sawmill, since it was eating up his savings and bringing nothing in. Thanks to his truck, he found a good job as a wood hauler for a big sawmill on the continent. Later, he will buy his own sawmill on the continent and go into business for himself. He wants to start over. He says there is no future for me in Oât. He is asking me to leave for the continent with him. He says again that he's very happy with me and that he wants to live with me on the continent in his truck, and later in his sawmill. I told the driver the truth. I like his truck very much, but I do not want to go and live on the continent. I can't abandon Mellie who expects me to visit her in the hospital every Thursday, and I can't abandon Nem either, even if he never notices me. And I do not want to leave Oât. The truck driver didn't understand. He says he is very disappointed in me, what good does it do to have the highest score on the test for the certificate if you only end up as the secretary in the municipal offices of Oât. That's not the way I seemed when he first saw me on the road. He thought I would go far, and I don't want to go any farther than Oât. You can hear the reproach in his voice. All the same, he gave me his address on the continent, at the sawmill where he will be picking up wood, just in case I change my mind. He says I am finished unless I change my mind. He thinks he knows me because we were together on the bunk in his truck. I have nothing else to say to him. Our walk along the beach ended there. The walk was ruined. My whole afternoon is ruined.

When we got back into the cab of the truck, even though the driver was angry, he wanted to push the button on the seat to turn it into a bunk one last time. I stopped him. The truck driver is a stranger to me now that he is leaving for the continent. I don't want him to touch me anymore. There is a fresh blood stain on the seat cover and another stain on my dress. But red on red doesn't show. I was right to wear my red velvet dress even if it did not bring me luck a second time. The driver started up, and he pushed the accelerator all the way down until we arrived in Oât. When we left each other, I wished him good luck. He did not wish me anything at all. He didn't even take one last look at me. He is in complete disagreement with me about everything. When the yellow truck disappeared at the end of the boulevard, I let the address the driver had given me blow away. I watched it fly off over the ocean. I don't want to keep the address on the continent.

I walked back down the boulevard to the fishing port. I will never see the yellow truck again. I sat on the dock. The Queen of the Fairies is still not back. Yem left a long time ago now. I don't want to go back to Nem's house. Suddenly I wanted to go back to Mellie's. I haven't been back there since she went to the hospital. I have the key, since the key that opens Nem's house also opens Mellie's house. It is dark in Mellie's house now that the second-hand man has taken away all the lamps. The rooms are empty. The walls are lighter where the mirrors were. I went into room 3. Night fell. Rain began to fall as well. This Sunday afternoon with the truck driver has completely exhausted me. I lay down right on the floor and fell asleep. I heard someone calling Mellie very loudly. It echoed from room to room. In the end it even woke me up. It is daylight already. But there is no one in Mellie's house except me. It was in my dream that I heard someone calling Mellie very loudly. I spent all night in Rose's room in Mellie's house. This is the first night I have spent away from Nem's house since I came to Oât.

Nem is not in his room. He isn't anywhere in his house. He must already be in his boat on the lagoon. He goes there earlier and earlier. I went to Markers Street. Nem's boat is tied up just in front of the house. That is not like him. Usually he spends all his time in his boat on the lagoon. I went into the house and up to the bedroom. Nem is lying on the bed next to the bride. The groom has disappeared. I woke Nem up. He acted as if he didn't know me. He asked me what I was doing in Rose's house. He says this is Rose's house. He seems exhausted but happy. He says he does not need anything now. He wants to spend his final days in Rose's house. He says he has finished with the house on Charms Street. He asked me to leave.

When I was back on Charms Street, I realized I could no longer live there now that Nem had left. So I took down the sign from the Hermitage and I put it back in my bag. I took my bag and the painting Mellie gave me, and I came back to Charms Way. This is not Mellie's house anymore, now that the house is empty and Mellie is in the hospital. I moved into room 3. But I feel as out of place in this empty house as in Nem's old house. I thought of Rose again. What was she thinking when she wrote the address on the last page of the book of legends? No one lives at 7 Charms Street now.

I can't get to sleep at night. So I go to the fishing port and sit on the dock. Tonight, the Queen of the Fairies is back. So Yem is back too. There are no lights on the deck or in the cabin. But there is a lamppost on the pier just in front of the boat, and it lights everything up. It is still the same little boat, but it has been painted white. White is not a color for a fishing boat. The name was also repainted, in big shiny black letters. I sat there for a long time looking at the Queen of the Fairies. Yem did not appear as I had hoped. So I walked up the boulevard to the Dance Palace, which was all lit up. For a minute, I wanted to go in. But I remembered the promise I made to the truck driver. A promise is a promise. I did not go into the Dance Palace, I walked back down the boulevard. I sat down again on the dock. I got my polaroid out of my bag and with my polaroid I photographed the Queen of the Fairies. It's a good thing there is a flash built into the polaroid. The photographer was not lying when he said it was the most advanced model. It's a very beautiful photo with the lamppost in the foreground lighting up the Queen of the Fairies' white hull with its black letters. On the back of the photo, I wrote: *The Queen of the Fairies at night in the port, back from a long voyage to Ot.* The lampposts of the port all went dark at once. It must be very late. I lost track of time. I walked up the boulevard again to the Dance Palace, and I photographed it as well. The Dance Palace is so brightly lit that the photo looks like nothing but spots of light. All the windows are lit up, there are lanterns everywhere on the terrace, and above it all the big flashing green neon sign: Dance Palace, which attracts sailors like a lighthouse in the dark. On the back of the photo I wrote in tiny letters because there is a lot to write: *The Dance Palace lit up in the darkness, where I will never go because I promised the truck driver on Seagull Beach the day before he left for the continent.* Beyond the Dance Palace, the Continental is completely dark. It has just closed indefinitely.

Back in my room, room 3, Rose's room, I spent a long time looking at my two new photos. Then I put them away in my book of legends. I am glad I took these two photos. My book of legends is always closed now. I wanted to reread The Queen of the Fairies to celebrate her return. But the old alphabet is less familiar to me now that I read the new alphabet all the time. I fell asleep in the middle of my reading.

Miss Martha resigned from her position as mayor. She has accepted a job as head of the Blue Island. The mayor's position is vacant. I walked Miss Martha to her boat. It reminded me of the night I did the same with Pim. This is the first time Miss Martha has been on a boat and her first trip to the continent. She made herself pretty. She is wearing a white suit with blue lapels. She wants to make a good impression when she gets to the Blue Island. She is leaving full of hope. Our goodbyes were brief. Miss Martha is in a hurry to get on board. She told me I was capable of getting along on my own now. I have proven myself in the municipal offices. Miss Martha hopes I will have my permanent appointment soon. For the moment I am still on probation. Miss Martha didn't want me to stay on the pier waiting for the boat to leave. As soon as she was on the deck, she looked out to sea in the direction of the continent. She gave me the address of the Blue Island, but she did not tell me to come and join her. The Blue Island is undoubtedly forbidden to minors. I stayed on the pier anyway and watched Miss Martha. When the boat raised anchor, I threw away the address of the Blue Island. The address flew away over the ocean like the truck driver's. I will never go to the continent.

I went back to Markers Street to see how Nem was. The house is empty. Nem is not in the bedroom and the bride is no longer lying on the bed. I found the groom at the back of the closet where Nem had hidden him. I looked out the window at the lagoon, hoping to see Nem's boat. But there are no boats on the lagoon. And Nem's boat is not tied up in front of the house. Nem must have wanted to go out in his boat one last time. He took the bride with him. The boat was old and rotting. It must have taken in water. Nem and the bride sank with the boat. Maybe that was what Nem wanted, to disappear at the bottom of the lagoon. The big rusty ship is half submerged. Only the rear deck is visible now. You wonder how the rear deck can stay above water at such a steep angle. Nem disappeared without leaving me a message, without leaving me anything. I laid the groom down on the bed. The groom is all alone now.

In the municipal offices, I did not record Nem's death. After all, I haven't seen him dead. He has only disappeared into the lagoon. Rose's death was not recorded either. There is nothing more for me to do in the office of records if I stop recording deaths. The municipal offices have been empty since Miss Martha left. Not a single citizen of Oât wants to be mayor. I wonder if I would want to replace Miss Martha if I was an adult. I don't think so. I am not cut out to be mayor. There is no question of that at my age anyway. I don't know if I will keep my job now that Miss Martha has left for the continent. Apparently there will no longer be a mayor in Oât. Oât will be annexed by the Municipality on the continent. There will be a representative of the continent in Oât instead of a mayor. That may be what the remaining citizens of Oât want.

Mellie's bed is empty. The nurse told me Mellie was dead. She died the day Nem disappeared into the lagoon. I asked the nurse where Mellie was buried. She pointed to the part of the vacant land that had not been flooded. The flooded part of the vacant land is the old cemetery of Oât. I didn't record Mellie's death either. I tore the last page out of the register of deaths. It was the only page that wasn't full. I don't want to work in the office of records anymore.

§9

I left Charms Way. Without Mellie, the house is unin-habitable. The secondhand man suggested I come and live in Miss Martha's lodgings. He is acting as mayor until an official representative of the continent is appointed to Oât. The secondhand man appointed me probationary copying clerk, like I wanted. He recognizes my abilities. I was trained by Miss Martha. My lodgings suit me very well. I live in the big sunny room that overlooks the ocean. I finally unwrapped Mellie's painting and I hung it on the wall facing the window. This is the first time I can look at it in natural light. At Mellie's, you could only look at it by lamplight. The secondhand man came to visit me to see if I have settled into my new lodgings. He was very surprised to see Mellie's painting. He had never seen it before. He recognized it right away. He says it is a copy of a painting in the Museum on the continent. The painter and the model are unknown. The secondhand man says it's a bad copy, and unfaithful to the original. So it is not a portrait of Rose as Mellie thought. Mellie would have been very disappointed to learn that her painting is a copy of a painting in the Museum on the continent. I trust the secondhand man. He knows about painting and he is very familiar with the Museum on the continent. He regularly goes to the continent on business and to oversee the construction of his house. I don't know what to think of Mellie's painting now that I know it is a copy and a bad one at that. Sometimes, when I look at myself in the mirror, I have the impression that I look like the model in the painting. That's all in my imagination. Mirrors are deceptive. I spend so much time looking at Mellie's painting and looking at myself in the mirror that in the end I get them mixed up. It's the same thing with names. Sometimes I don't know who Mellie is. Mellie is me. I must not forget that. Fortunately I have my identity card with my photo glued to it. There is no doubt, my name is Mellie. But I no longer live at 7 Charms Street like Miss Martha wrote on my identity card. I asked the secondhand man to write my new address on my identity card so it would be up to date. He told me he does not have the authority to do that, but that the address is of no importance anyway.

Now that I am a copying clerk, the fishermen come and see me in the municipal offices. My certificate impresses them. They dictate letters to the Municipality of the continent. We have been having rains like Oât has not seen for a long time. The waters of the lagoon rose very suddenly and flooded the entire lagoon neighborhood, where the fishermen live. The fishermen are homeless. In their letters, they ask for authorization to live in the empty houses of the Charms neighborhood, which is not flooded. The fisher- men say they have never seen such a flood. The vacant land has disappeared since it was flooded. The vacant land is like the lagoon now. The water stops just alongside the road that links the city to the port. It's a miracle that the road is floodproof.

The secondhand man still wants to exchange his case of jewels for my sign from the Hermitage. And yet he knows I will never part with my sign, even if it pains me not to have the case of jewels. They are exactly the jewels I would like to wear. The secondhand man explained why he is so interested in my sign. In the old days, in a little alleyway in the Charms neighborhood just behind Wardens Square, there was a souvenir shop with a sign exactly like mine. It's a sign that does not look like the signs you see in Oât. The secondhand man says he does not know where it came from, but that he is sure it is not from Oât. It was while he was looking around in that souvenir shop that he found the case of jewels, and that was when he decided to become a secondhand man. And then one day the shop closed and the sign disappeared. Ever since then, the secondhand man has been trying to find the sign. And here he is saying that it is in my possession. I understand the secondhand man better now. He grows on you. He finally realized that I would not sell him my sign, and he is not angry with me. I asked him who ran the souvenir shop. He remembers that it was a very old woman, but he doesn't remember if her name was Rose or Mellie. I did not put the sign from the Hermitage up in my new lodgings. You must not mix old and new. I keep my sign on my nightstand, within reach so I can look at it at night before I go to sleep. I no longer need to reread my book of legends. I only need to read Souvenir Shop written in the old alphabet on the sign from the Hermitage. The secondhand man can't have everything. He bought up all the signs from the Charms neighborhood.

The Queen of the Fairies is never in the harbor when I go and sit on the dock. And yet she is back, since I photographed her the evening of her return. A fisherman told me she came back to the port very late at night after all the fishing boats, long after I was in bed. The water level in the lagoon has begun to drop. But the vacant land is still flooded. The lagoon covers the vacant land, it almost completely surrounds Oât now. The Municipality of the continent authorized the fishermen to live in the Charms neighborhood. The houses in the lagoon neighborhood are still flooded. The fishermen will not miss their houses.

I have just turned fourteen. I feel like time is passing more and more quickly. For my birthday, I wanted to go back and see the tree blooming in the courtyard of Nem's old house. It blooms just around the time of my birthday. But the tree had not bloomed. It's dying. The roots must have been drowned with all the rain that fell. The tree is very old, it could not withstand that. The courtyard looks desolate now that the tree is dying. In my old room, there is still the little bed, the writing desk, and the bookshelf. It's the only room at 7 Charms Street that is not empty. 75

The secondhand man doesn't care that the lagoon neighborhood is flooded. To him, Oât is only Wardens Square. The secondhand man can say that there is nothing left to buy in Oât and nothing left to do, but he still has not made up his mind to go and live on the continent in his unfinished house. He doesn't want to be idle. So he began repainting the facades of the old administrative buildings on Wardens Square. The square had a sad look about it with its dilapidated facades. The secondhand man's idea of repainting them was a good one. He is repainting all the facades pink. He is proud of his work. He installed a bench in the middle of the square and he sits there contemplating the facades that he has just repainted. It's a pleasant surprise to come upon Wardens Square now that the secondhand man has repainted it. It looks brand-new. The secondhand man invites me to sit down on the bench next to him. He has taken me into his care. He tells me about his house on the continent. He says he furnished it with the most beautiful things he bought in Oât from the houses in the Charms neighborhood. He is wondering if he shouldn't turn his house on the continent into a museum of Oât. It's funny how fond they are of museums. The photographer wants to found a museum in Oât with his collection of old cameras from the continent, and the secondhand man wants to turn his house on the continent into a museum of Oât.

The photographer seems much older. He cannot get over the fact that Miss Martha chose to become the head of the Blue Island instead of the curator of the museum in Oât. Before she left, he offered to open the museum right away, without waiting to complete his collection. But Miss Martha refused. Ever since then, the photographer has been crushed. He no longer even wants to complete his collection or found a museum in Oât. The photographer told me the news from Miss Martha. He hears from her regularly. The latest news is not good. The success of the Blue Island was short-lived. The Blue Island is going to close. So Miss Martha failed in her position as head of the Blue Island. Little by little her clientele was tempted away by the growing prestige of the Dance Palace. The Dance Palace is going to triumph over the Blue Island like it triumphed over the Continental. The photographer even says that it is only thanks to the Dance Palace that people still come to the port. Ships schedule a stop at Oât just for a night at the Dance Palace. The photographer says Miss Martha is finished now. He cannot bear to look at his cameras anymore. He put them away in crates. I go to see him regularly to keep him company. I never forget that he gave me the polaroid. The secondhand man suggested that he sell his collection to the Museum on the continent. He says it is a lovely collection even if it isn't complete. Miss Martha was wrong to scoff at it. The photographer agreed to sell his collection. He trusts the secondhand man. He says his collection was for nothing. He has a new project. He wants there to be no more Storks Street in Oât. So he is going to have his house demolished. He says Storks Street should never have been in the middle of the Charms neighborhood. It was bad planning. The secondhand man invited the photographer to come and live in his house, which is too big for him. The photographer accepted the secondhand man's offer. He says he appreciates Wardens Square now that the secondhand man has repainted it pink. You would never think the administrative buildings of Oât used to be on Wardens Square. The pink houses do not make you think of administrative buildings. It is as if Oât had a new square all of a sudden. The photographer says the secondhand man should have been a painter and he himself should have been an architect, he says they both missed their calling. He hired two builders to demolish his house. I photographed the photographer's house before the two builders began demolishing it. The house is in the very center of the photo. On the back of the photo, I wrote: *1 Storks Street in the middle of the Charms neighborhood, the house of the photographer before its demolition.*

The skipper of the Queen of the Fairies is sitting on the dock. But the Queen of the Fairies is still not in the harbor. I couldn't stop myself from asking him for news of Yem. He would like nothing better than to tell me about

Yem. He wants me to call him by his name, Cob. Cob is not a name from here, it is a name that comes from Ot.

Cob's ancestors come from Ot. Ever since he got back from his long voyage, Cob says he feels dizzy as soon as he puts out to sea. So Yem goes and fishes alone and looks after the Queen of the Fairies in Cob's place. Cob says Yem is a better sailor now than he is. Yem became a real sailor during the long voyage to Ot. Cob had always dreamt of that voyage. But with his little boat, he hesitated. He is not sorry he went to Ot, even if he came back with dizzy spells. Now he knows the Queen of the Fairies is not a boat like the others. That was just what the former owner of the Queen of the Fairies told him when he bought it, but Cob didn't really believe him. Cob never saw the former owner of the Queen of the Fairies again. He was a foreigner. He left just after the sale. Now Cob has proof that he wasn't lying to him when he told him about the unique qualities of the Queen of the Fairies. During the voyage, the Queen of the Fairies weathered many storms, and with no damage. Cob and Yem had good catches. They made a great deal of money. Before coming back to Oât, Cob had the Queen of the Fairies painted white so it wouldn't look like a fishing boat anymore, even though it still is a fishing boat.

Cob is even more eager to tell me what is happening now. He says Yem is doing something that no fisherman from Oât has ever done. Yem did not want to go back and fish where the fishermen from Oât go. He decided to go and fish alone on the northern coast in the middle of the shoals. Cob wanted to stop Yem because the northern coast has a dark reputation among the sailors. But Yem would not hear of it. Cob thinks it is the Queen of the Fairies that is making Yem so fearless. Yem can make her do anything he wants. And his bet paid off. Every night after midnight he comes back to the port with his hold full of big beautiful fish. At dawn, he sets out again to fish off the northern coast. And every night after midnight, Cob waits for Yem on the dock. Yem gives him his catch. In the morning, Cob enjoys the admiration and envy of all the fishermen of Oât as he goes to market to sell Yem's catch. Cob says Yem is protected from harm because the Queen of the Fairies is stronger than the ocean and its shoals. He is wondering what to buy with all the money he makes selling Yem's catch. He has never had so much money. He does not think he would have been as fearless as Yem at his age, but he thinks that it's thanks to him and their voyage together to Ot that Yem is so fearless. Now I understand why the Queen of the Fairies is never there when I come and sit on the dock. Cob told me that I will have to be on the pier after midnight if I want to see Yem.

§10

Yem kept the promise he made to me the day I met him. He let me come on board the Queen of the Fairies. I got there just after midnight like Cob told me. This is the first time I have been on a boat. You can hardly tell you are not on land anymore but on water. Yem still lives in the little cabin under the deck. It's a cabin for just one person with a narrow and uncomfortable bunk. Yem and I sat down on the bunk. Yem lit the lamp. I saw him clearly then. I think he has changed a great deal. His face is lined for his age and he looks very tired. He says when he returns from fishing at night he sleeps very soundly, fully dressed on his bunk. He feels like he has died when he sleeps. Every night, he feels like he has died. But he says life returns to him at dawn when he raises anchor and leaves the port.

Yem opened a bottle of sparkling wine. This is the first time I have tasted it. Yem told me to make a wish since this was the first time I have been on a boat and have drunk sparkling wine. I made the wish right away, without thinking: a long and happy life for the Queen of the Fairies. That was the only wish that occurred to me. I asked Yem if he had made a wish too. He says he made one on the night when he drank sparkling wine for the first time. It was with Cob, the night before they left for Ot. Yem did not tell me what his wish was. That's his secret. He asked me to tell him about my life in Oât. I told him everything except what happened with the truck driver and with Pim. Then Yem told me about himself. My head spins a little faster every time Yem pours me more of the wine, which is wonderful to drink, with all its bubbles. I have the impression that Yem's voice is coming from very far away. Yem tells me everything Cob told me. The Queen of the Fairies cannot sink because she is made differently from other boats. Yem also told me about the channel he discovered on the northern coast in the middle of the shoals. He did not tell Cob about it. He made me promise not to tell him about it. He is only talking about it to me. It's a very narrow channel that only a boat as small as the Queen of the Fairies can follow. You would think the channel was made especially for the Queen of the Fairies. Yem thinks the reason no sailor has ever discovered it before is that it's invisible until you enter the area of the shoals, and Yem says sailors never enter the area of the shoals. I like to listen to Yem talk. His voice is coming to me more and more faintly. I fell asleep while I was listening to him, just like he must have fallen asleep while he was talking to me. At dawn, he woke me up. We slept side by side fully dressed on the narrow bunk. I asked Yem to take me with him to the northern coast into the middle of the shoals. But he refused. He fishes alone. So I climbed down onto the pier, and I watched him leave.

Every night after midnight I am on the pier with Cob, and I see the Queen of the Fairies coming into the port. And every night I sleep beside Yem in the tiny cabin. Yem always comes back from fishing so exhausted that he falls asleep as soon as he lies down on the bunk. For me, it is as if he were dead. I would like to be able to wake him up, but he really needs to sleep and regain his strength. Ever since I started sleeping beside Yem, I have been sleeping lightly. At dawn, when Yem comes back to life, it's only so he can set off for more fishing with the Queen of the Fairies.

Yem wanted us to become engaged on my birthday. I am fifteen. He gave me an engagement present. He bought the case of jewels from the secondhand man, the jewels I had told him about so many times. There is no more beautiful gift he could have given me. The secondhand man is attached to me, that was why he agreed to sell Yem the jewel case that he was so proud of. And on the day I turned fifteen which was also the day of my engagement, I put on all the jewels in the case except one. I have never worn jewels before, and here I am covered with them. Yem told me I should always wear them because now they are a part of me. I didn't dare tell him that they are too beautiful for me.

With the rest of his money, Yem bought a little piece of land running along the boulevard next to the fishing port. He wants to build his house there. He says the two of us can't go on forever sleeping on the narrow bunk in his cabin. This is the first time Yem has thought of sleeping in a house and not on a boat. The house will face the ocean, just a few yards away from the Queen of the Fairies. Yem said we would be married as soon as the house is built. He asked me to choose the design of the house, but to make sure it has a good foundation. I thought about the photographer. I will give him a chance to show his skill as an architect. The photographer has moved into the secondhand man's house. The two builders are demolishing the house on Storks Street. I went to see the two builders to ask them if they would be willing to build our house when they have finished demolishing the photographer's house. They agreed right away. The photographer is willing to design it on the condition that he can take as long as he needs. He says he wants to make a perfect design.

Yem thinks he is unbeatable. Every night he comes back with his boat loaded with crates of big fish. He earns a lot of money, which he shares with Cob. They split it evenly. Yem gave the builders an advance so they will begin working on the excavation as soon as they have finished demolishing the photographer's house. It was built so solidly that it's taking them forever to demolish it. The photographer finished his design. It is exactly the same design as the house on Storks Street. The photographer said he tried other designs, but this was the only one that really satisfied him. I took the photographer's design to the builders. They need the design so they can start the excavation.

Yem asked Cob to sell him the Queen of the Fairies. It is no longer enough for him to have her all to himself, he also wants to be the owner. Cob said he wanted to think about it. But he will agree, since he wants to retire. Yem comes back more exhausted every night. He works harder and harder at fishing. He needs a great deal of money to pay for the boat and the house. It is beyond his strength to go on fishing this way.

Oât was officially annexed by the Municipality on the continent. The secondhand man was officially named representative of the continent in Oât. He was tailor-made for the position, since he lives in Oât and has a house on the continent. The municipal offices in the port were closed. The secondhand man opened his office as representative of the continent in the freshly painted Wardens Square, on the ground floor of his big house. He put in a little office for me next to his. I am still the copying clerk. I still write letters, now they are administrative letters between Oât and the continent. The secondhand man takes his official functions very seriously.

Ever since his house was demolished, the photographer says he wants to forget Storks Street. The sign that said Storks Street was taken down. There is no more Storks Street. The photographer lives in a little room on the second floor of the secondhand man's house. He only wants to live in one room. He didn't bring anything with him. His collection of old cameras was sold to the Museum on the continent for a good price. The photographer never talks about it. It is as if he had never had a collection. Where Storks Street used to be in the middle of the Charms neighborhood, now there is an empty space. I asked the photographer to take our picture, Yem and me, by the site of our new house. It's up to him to take the photo because he is the architect. The builders have just begun the excavation. The photographer says this will be his last photo. Yem looks tall next to me in the photo. I am not as tall as I thought. I must have stopped growing when I was twelve years old. In the photo, Yem's eyes and the stones in my jewelry are the same shade of blue. On the back of the photo, I wrote: *Yem and Mellie during their engagement in front of the site of their future house by the sea, the first day of the excavation.* I put my new photo in my book of legends. 85

The Customs office was enlarged. Now it takes up the space that the old municipal offices used to occupy. I still have my lodgings on the top floor. But I am never there. I have nothing to do there. I hardly recognize Mellie's painting anymore. It surely wasn't made to be exposed to sunlight. All the colors are disappearing. You can just barely make out the model. The girl's features are almost gone. I spend my days in my little office on Wardens Square and my nights in the cabin of the Queen of the Fairies. Yem's sleep is more and more troubled. Yem is wondering why his catches aren't as good as they used to be not so long ago. He is still fishing just as energetically. But he says there are fewer fish on the northern coast of Oât. He is pushing farther into the channel in hopes of finding the big fish again. But he has the impression that there are not many fish in the channel. He is agitated. He is trying to understand what is happening, but he does not understand. And yet he should be happy. He is the owner of the Queen of the Fairies now. Cob sold it to him for the price he paid for it. It's a lovely gift he has given to Yem.

Cob has just decided what he is going to buy with his money. He wants to build a bungalow on Seagull Beach. He has always liked that beach. Now that he has sold the

Queen of the Fairies, he wants to spend his last days there. Since he is suddenly in a hurry to live there, he chose to

have a bungalow built because he says they are the quickest thing to build and they don't need a foundation. Cob does not see the point of foundations in the sand. His bungalow arrived on a boat from the continent, in separate pieces. They only need to be put together. Every day, Cob goes to Seagull Beach to oversee the construction of his bungalow. He bought himself a little boat to go to Seagull Beach in. But he says the boat is too tiring, he is too old for it. So he bought himself a car to come and go from the beach to the port. Cob is proud of his car. It's a used Buick, covered with chrome. It also came directly from the continent. Cob never gets tired of looking at his Buick.

Cob had to take the test for a driver's license to drive the Buick. The fishermen of Oât don't have driver's licenses because they don't have cars. Cob takes me for drives in his Buick. We make round-trips without stopping from the beach to the port and from the port to the beach. It's a Buick convertible. Cob likes to put the top up and down. Even though the Buick is an old model, it is still very advanced. To put the top up or down, all you have to do is push a button. Driving in the Buick with Cob is intoxicating. It makes me forget Yem's worries. The hold is not as full of fish as before, but it is still full enough. I share in Cob's happiness.

I look forward to Sunday all week long, even more than I look forward to after midnight during the week. Yem never goes fishing on Sundays. On Sundays, he takes me for a little cruise on the ocean. Yem does not want to take me to the northern coast where he fishes. He takes me to the southern coast because the ocean is always calm there. I stay on deck next to Yem. We go far out to sea, until Oât is no longer visible.

In the afternoon, we go to visit Cob on Seagull Beach. He waits for us. He is happy to see the Queen of the Fairies every Sunday. Yem throws out the anchor when we are just in front of Cob's bungalow, and then we go to the beach in the little rubber life raft. Yem taught me to row. Yem always puts the life raft away on the beach next to Cob's boat. Cob never uses his boat anymore, now that he has his Buick. He has set up big fishing poles in front of his bungalow, and sits on his porch watching over them from morning to evening. He says he catches many fish.

Yem and I walk along the beach. We turn around to look at the Queen of the Fairies. The letters are shiny black against the white hull. Yem bought new sails of an immaculate white. Looking at it from Seagull Beach, you might think the Queen of the Fairies was a little pleasure craft. In the cabin, above the bunk, I carved our two names: Yem and Mellie. Yem said I had damaged the varnished wood. On Sundays, it is as if the week didn't exist.

I photographed Cob in front of his bungalow. In the photo, the bungalow looks tiny compared to the beach, and Cob also looks tiny sitting on the porch. That's because I took the photo from very far away so you can really see the beach with the flocks of seagulls squeezed right up against each other. The bungalow is the same blue as the

ocean. On the back of the photo, I wrote: *The blue bungalow built by Cob, the former owner of the Queen of the Fairies, on Seagull Beach.*

Yem and I finish the afternoon in the Buick. The keys are in the ignition. Neither Yem nor I know how to drive. We don't want to drive, we only want to be in the Buick. We put the top up so we will be sheltered. We lie down on the back seat. It's much bigger and more comfortable than the bunk in the Queen of the Fairies. It's a real seat for two. It gets hot in the Buick when you put the top up. Yem and I feel like we are taking a trip without moving. Cob is always on the porch watching over his fishing poles and looking at the Queen of the Fairies. I asked him to photograph Yem and me in the Buick. Cob did not center the photo properly. All you can see is the front of the Buick from very close up. That's all you can see in the picture, which is cut off just before the windshield. So you cannot see Yem and Mellie in the Buick. I told Cob his photo was a success so that he wouldn't feel bad. He does not understand anything about centering a photo. On the back of the photo, I wrote: *The front of the Buick, and Yem and Mellie invisible in the back seat.*

§11

The Dance Palace is full every night. It's so brightly lit that it illuminates the whole port. Apparently you have to make reservations far in advance. Walking in front of the Dance Palace at midnight, I thought I saw Miss Martha on the terrace. The photographer is the only one who could tell me if it really was Miss Martha I thought I saw on the terrace of the Dance Palace. The photographer is becoming quieter and quieter. The shutters of his room are closed. He never comes out onto Wardens Square. I am afraid he might be sick. He has been looking unwell ever since his house was demolished and he says he has forgotten about Storks Street.

When I went into the photographer's room, I found him sitting in his armchair, in the dark. He did not want me to open the shutters. I had to talk to him in the dark. He took a long time answering when I asked him if that really was Miss Martha I·thought I saw on the terrace of the Dance Palace. After the Blue Island closed, Miss Martha felt like she was in exile on the continent. So she too finally gave in to the attraction of the Dance Palace. The photographer says they hired her for the lowliest job, the one that is the most unworthy of her. Now she lives at the Dance Palace day and night. The photographer also says Miss Martha is ill. He says that she fell ill a little while after she moved to the continent. It is a hopeless and incurable disease. The photographer asked me not to come and see him in his room again. He does not want to talk about Miss Martha anymore, and when he sees me he cannot help talking about her. He wants to live alone.

I did not go to the Dance Palace to see Miss Martha. I

don't know how she would have received me. I don't think she wants to see me again. And then, I have to keep my promise. I promised never to go back to the Dance Palace. I have forgotten about the truck driver, but not about my promise. Yem would not understand if he learned that I had been to the Dance Palace. I have never told Yem about Miss Martha.

The flooding is over. But the vacant land is still almost completely covered with water, except where the road is. The lagoon neighborhood is like a ghost town. The houses were very seriously damaged, they are in danger of collapsing. The fishermen will not be able to move back into their old houses. They are going to go on living in the Charms neighborhood. The Charms neighborhood isn't the Charms neighborhood anymore. Markers Street is barely recognizable. It is as if there had been a cataclysm. The house on Markers Street was carried away by the violence of the rising waters. Even though its facade was made of stone, it was less solid than it looked. There are no houses left on Markers Street. It is not even a street anymore. The groom must have been reunited with the bride somewhere at the bottom of the lagoon. In the end, the big rusty ship became completely submerged. The lagoon looks empty. I don't know why I come back to this deserted neighborhood. Maybe it's because of the mountains of the Hermitage, which I can see in the distance when the clouds lift. I try to remember the house by the falls. I have the impression that everything is fading away. Yem says I should not spend my time at the edge of the lagoon. But after all, he goes into the channel with the Queen of the Fairies.

Every day, I go by and see the builders who are doing the excavation for our future house. They are digging deep, like Yem wanted and like it says in the photographer's design. It will be a stone house, like the old house on Storks Street. I am in a hurry for the builders to stop digging and start building the house. I am more and more worried about Yem. Some nights, the Queen of the Fairies doesn't come back to the port. Yem went too far into the channel and didn't have time to make it back. I don't like to think of him so far from the port at night. The fish are still disappearing. I wait for Yem every night after midnight, not knowing whether or not he will come back. Now that Cob lives on Seagull Beach, I am the one who goes and sells the fish at market. Every time they give me a smaller amount in exchange for Yem's catch. When Yem comes back to the port, he is so gloomy that he hardly notices me waiting for him on the dock. He never stops wondering why there are no fish in the channel. I asked him why he doesn't go and fish where the other fishermen of Oât fish. Yem answered that he would never go and fish with the fishermen of Oât because the Queen of the Fairies is not a fishing boat like all the rest. Yem is far away. He almost never sleeps at night anymore. He tosses and turns in his bunk.

The builders finally finished the excavation. They asked Yem for another advance so they could start the foundation. But Yem has nothing to give them now that he hardly makes any money. So the builders said they wouldn't work without an advance, and they decided to stop the construction. I don't know when I will see our house rise up out of the ground. I no longer feel at home in the lodgings in the old municipal offices since the whole building became the property of the Customs office. The secondhand man gave me a room with a balcony in his house on Wardens Square. He thought I would be happy in the room, which has a panoramic view over the whole square. It's next door to the photographer's room. The secondhand man understood my worries and my disappointment, even though I never tell him about them. I brought all my things to my new room. I still sleep beside Yem when the Queen of the Fairies comes back to the port, but I have not moved my things into the cabin. There is no room, and Yem never asked me to. On the wall of my new room, across from the balcony, I put up Mellie's painting. The painting could not withstand the light in my old lodgings. All the colors, and even the model, have disappeared. You can no longer tell that Mellie's painting was a copy of a painting in the Museum on the continent. You can't see anything at all anymore when you look at the painting. I photographed it the way it is now. You can see a big white spot on the photo. On the back of the photo, I wrote: *Mellie's big white painting.*

I will never forget this Sunday. Yem and I went for our sail on the ocean, and then we went to see Cob on Seagull Beach like every Sunday. Yem brought along a bottle of sparkling wine to drink in the Buick. He is as happy as if he had just brought in his best catch ever. And yet yesterday he came back to the port before midnight with his hold completely empty, and he announced that he was giving up fishing. He does not seem crushed at the thought of giving it up, on the contrary, it is as if he had been liberated. Yem did not say what he is going to do now that he has given up fishing. We drank the entire bottle of sparkling wine. Our heads are spinning more and more. It is as if there was no such thing as the Queen of the Fairies anymore. The Buick is also beginning to spin. And with the Buick spinning faster and faster, Yem asked me to marry him. I thought he didn't want to get married until the house was finished. But he says he has changed his mind. He wants us to get married now. He says we have been engaged long enough. So the sparkling wine was to celebrate his marriage proposal. He asked me to forgive him for not having the money to buy me a wedding present. I told him the case of jewels was an engagement present and a wedding present.

Cob was moved when Yem announced that we were going to be married. He has not been to the port for some time. But he says he will go back for our wedding. He wants to be our first witness. He started the engine in the Buick to make sure it was still running. He doesn't want to drive anymore because he never wants to leave the porch of his bungalow, where he feels so comfortable. So he forgets to maintain the Buick. There is sand coming in under the hood. Cob knows nothing about engines. Even though Seagull Beach is sheltered, when the wind blows it picks up the sand and the sand works its way under the hood of the Buick. Sand is bad for the engine. The chrome is beginning to get rust spots. Cob thinks the Buick is just fine as it is. He says he has nothing to worry about, since the engine runs.

The secondhand man married us two days later. This is his first wedding since he became the official representative of the continent in Oât. He took the marriage ceremony very seriously. He did everything he could to get the photographer to participate. The photographer finally gave in, even though he had sworn never to leave his room again. He was our second witness, after Cob. I know that while he was participating in my wedding he was thinking of Miss Martha who never married, and he was also thinking of the life she leads now every day and night at the Dance Palace. I thought about Miss Martha for a moment too. But I quickly forgot about her. This is my wedding day. The secondhand man married us on the deck of the Queen of the Fairies, like Yem wanted. In my jewel case, there is one jewel I have never worn. It is a very old ring. That will be my wedding present. Yem put it on my finger. It's just the right size for my finger. I will never take it off. There is no ring for Yem.

Yem wanted to photograph me in my wedding dress on the deck of the Queen of the Fairies. It's the last photo left in the polaroid. I wanted Yem to photograph me in front of our future house. There is a big hole dug in the ground now that the excavation is finished. My wedding dress is the secondhand man's wedding present to me. It's a satin and lace dress, with a long train. It is an old dress that has never been worn. The secondhand man had kept it to give to his fiancée on the day of their wedding, but he was never engaged. This is the first time I have worn a long dress with a train. The secondhand man says a wedding dress should only be worn for twenty-four hours. He wanted to give Yem a groom's suit, but the suit did not fit him. So Yem was married in his Sunday suit, a sailor's suit with gold buttons. Yem is using the polaroid for the first time. He centered the photo very precisely so you can see the excavation for our future house and also the Queen of the Fairies in the background. He put me in the foreground. I am a little blurry in the photo because of the net veil hiding my face and ruffling a little in the wind. On the back of the photo Yem gave me, I wrote: *Mellie photographed by Yem the day of their wedding in front of the completed excavation of their future house with the Queen of the Fairies in the background.* I am sorry that Yem is not next to me in the photo. But he said it was up to him to take the last photo. And he could not be in the photo and take the photo at the same time. The photographer was not there anymore when Yem photographed me.

I spent my wedding night with Yem in the cabin of the Queen of the Fairies. We didn't sleep all night. I kept my wedding dress on all night. Yem wanted me to keep it on. I will have worn it for twenty-four hours, just as long as the secondhand man said it should be worn. Yem talked all night. He told me he was going to leave on a very long voyage with the Queen of the Fairies. He never forgot his voyage to Ot with Cob. He says Ot is nothing like Oât. Yem wants to explore the channel, to follow it to the end. He wants to know where the channel goes. He says the Queen of the Fairies was made for the channel and he doesn't want to miss the opportunity he has been given. He says he came to understand that when the fish began to disappear. He no longer misses fishing. Yem waited for our wedding night to announce that he was leaving. I asked him to let me go with him. He said the Queen of the Fairies does not have room for two for such a long voyage. He said he would come back and that I had to wait for him. All night long, he told me about the voyage he will make as he follows the channel.

At dawn, like every other morning, I climbed down onto the pier, and I watched the Queen of the Fairies leave the port. After a while, Yem stopped looking at me and looked out to sea in the direction of the channel. But I went on standing on the pier in my wedding dress, trying to keep him in sight. I stayed there a long time looking at the ocean, long after the Queen of the Fairies had disappeared over the horizon. And then all of a sudden everything stopped. I had the impression that even the ocean had stopped moving.

I was still on the pier when the fishermen came. They asked me what I was doing there all alone in my wedding dress. So I told them about Yem's leaving and about the channel he wants to follow to the end. The fishermen shook their heads. They say the channel only exists in legends. They think I was wrong to marry Yem. But I do not think like they do. I was right to marry Yem, no matter what the fishermen think. They don't understand anything about the Queen of the Fairies.

My period is late. It has always been perfectly regular ever since I left the Hermitage. And now for the first time my period is late. I reread the pamphlet they gave me at the clinic. It says that when your period is late you have to go for an examination at the clinic right away. At the clinic, they examined me, they ran tests. Finally they said it was not just that my period was late, but that it had really stopped. That means I am pregnant. They gave me another pamphlet that explains everything that happens during the nine months of pregnancy. Nine months is a long time. I read and reread the pamphlet. I want to understand everything. This is the first time I have been pregnant. It is much more important than the first time I had my period.

Every day I walk by the site of our future house. For now, it is only an abandoned construction site with a big hole in the middle. I put up a sign in front of the excavation: Private property. And I wrote the names of the owners on the sign: Yem and Mellie. I like to walk by the sign where our names are written next to private property. Yem and I were married under the system of common property. The secondhand man carefully explained to us what that means. Everything I own belongs to Yem, and everything Yem owns belongs to me.

Every Sunday I go to Seagull Beach. I go on foot. It's a two-hour walk as long as you walk quickly. It makes me happy to walk quickly on the road that runs alongside the ocean. My body needs exercise. The walk does me good. I take deep breaths. Cob was not interested when I told him I was pregnant. And yet it's big news. But Cob never thinks about anything anymore but the Queen of the Fairies and Yem. I had to tell him all about the channel to explain the reasons why Yem went away. He has been absorbed in his thoughts ever since I told him about the channel. He says he wishes he were Yem and not Cob. He doesn't like Seagull Beach or his blue bungalow anymore. He says Yem was the only one who understood what to do with the Queen of the Fairies. It is the boat that was made for the channel. It was not a boat made for going to Ot or for fishing in the middle of the shoals. Cob used to be happy and now he isn't. He dreams as he sits by his fishing poles. He forgets to put the hooks on. He never even asks me how I am.

I spend my Sundays in the Buick. I go to Seagull Beach more for the Buick than for Cob, who acts as if I did not exist. He doesn't care about the Buick now. He is letting it rust and get filled in with sand everywhere. The tires have gone flat. I tried to start the engine. The engine has broken down. The Buick does not run anymore. The seagulls adore the Buick. They use it as a perch. They squeeze together on the hood and on the fenders. If I didn't put the top up, they would invade the inside. When I am in the Buick, the seagulls are there right against the windshield looking at me. I lie down on the back seat. After the walk, I need to lie down. I spend hours on the back seat looking at the sky and the seagulls. I have a humming in my head and ears.

I will never see Miss Martha again. She was found dead in the restrooms of the Dance Palace. It was the secondhand man who told me the bad news. So right up to the end Miss Martha frequented the restrooms. The secondhand man doesn't know how she died. He organized a memorial service in honor of what Miss Martha used to be and of the role she played in the municipal offices of the port. Apparently there was a large crowd on the terrace of the Dance Palace during the memorial service. The secondhand man told me about Miss Martha's death after the service, so I would not be overwhelmed. He says I have to avoid strong emotions in my condition. He knows that I was friends with Miss Martha. I often think now of Miss

Martha's sad end. I don't know the circumstances of her end, but in the restrooms of the Dance Palace it can only have been a sad end. The secondhand man says it was a shameful death. But Miss Martha's reputation was restored thanks to the memorial service, which paid tribute to her past as mayor. The secondhand man can't really understand Miss Martha, despite his desire to understand.

I have not seen the photographer since my wedding day. He was not at the memorial service. The shutters of his room are always closed. The photographer never goes out anymore. Even though I live in the room next to his, I never hear any noises. The secondhand man says the photographer has let himself go since Miss Martha died. Nothing can console him, since he is inconsolable. He lives alone in his dark room.

The secondhand man comes and goes between Oât and the continent. He has two lives and two houses. There is nothing left for him to buy in Oât, but he carefully manages the small fortune he made as a secondhand man. Thanks to him, Wardens Square looks brand-new. Nothing in Oât looks like Oât anymore. The lagoon neighborhood will never be inhabitable again. The Charms neighborhood has become the fishermen's neighborhood. Storks Street has disappeared. And Wardens Square no longer looks anything like the old Wardens Square. The secondhand man's house on the continent has officially become the museum of Oât, as he had planned. The museum is a success. The inhabitants of the continent know about Oât thanks to the secondhand man's museum. Everything of any value that used to be in the houses in the Charms neighborhood is now on display on the continent in the secondhand man's museum.

Sometimes sailors who have stopped at Oât talk to the fishermen about the Queen of the Fairies. They have seen it somewhere far from Oât, never in the same direction. There is no point in listening to what the sailors say. Yem is making his way along the channel. He said he would go to the end. If the channel exists in legends, that proves that it exists. The fishermen understand nothing about legends. Rose taught me to understand them. She understood them better than anyone. It was not for nothing that she taught me to read from her book of legends, and then gave it to me afterwards. That was her only present. The wish Yem made the first time he drank sparkling wine with Cob, the wish he never wanted to tell me because it was his secret, must have been to make this long voyage alone with the Queen of the Fairies, and to discover the channel he used to dream about before he discovered it. His wish was granted. I hope my wish will also be granted. The two wishes complement each other. Yem made his wish before he became engaged. A wish is sacred.

In my room on Wardens Square, I finally turned Mellie's painting to the wall. There is no point in keeping it right side out since there is nothing to see in it. Mellie had also turned it to the wall. It was enough for her that her painting be hung wrong side out on her parlor wall. I like my room when the sun sets. The sun comes into my room.

The light is all pink because of the facades that the secondhand man repainted and also because of the light of the setting sun. Just before night falls, it looks like I live in a pink room. The photographer has closed himself away forever in his dark room. There is no hope for him now.

Every month I go for a medical examination at the clinic. My silhouette is changing. My stomach is rounder and rounder. I do everything just the way they tell me to do it at the clinic. I take vitamin capsules. Every afternoon, I take a nap. I dream of Yem and the Queen of the Fairies.

On Sunday, Cob was in a state of great excitement when I got to his house. Off Seagull Beach, just facing his bungalow, there is a marvelous white yacht, the biggest yacht I have ever seen. Its name is written in blue letters: Queen of the Fairies. Cob took down his fishing poles from the beach because from his porch the poles were blocking the view of the Queen of the Fairies. He is completely transfixed to see the big yacht just facing his bungalow. He says he has been waiting for it forever, it's the Queen of the Fairies. He has forgotten Yem. I spent my Sunday lying down in the Buick, with my eyes closed. There is a party on board the yacht. I can hear the music even in the Buick. The music from the yacht lulls me. I dozed a long time in the Buick, with my eyes closed.

The next Sunday, Cob's bungalow was locked up. I looked everywhere for Cob. There is no trace of Cob on the beach or in the area. He disappeared without leaving me a fare- well note or an explanation. He only left me the Buick, half buried in sand. The yacht isn't anchored off Seagull Beach anymore. And Cob's boat is not on the beach.

§12

At my medical examination they told me it would be soon. The next time I come to the clinic, it will be for the delivery. They showed me my room. It's a white room overlooking the ocean. Everything is ready. There is a crib next to the bed. They gave me a new pamphlet to prepare me for the delivery. I have always been well looked after at the clinic. They told me my pregnancy was normal and that everything looked like it would be fine. The second-hand man put me on maternity leave. I no longer work at the office. My days are free. I rest a lot. Sometimes I go back to the edge of the lagoon now that it is no longer flooded. I cannot stop myself from going back there. I look off in the distance at the mountains of the Hermi-tage. From far away, they seem very close.

The idea came to me as I was going back to Wardens Square after walking along the edge of the lagoon. For my delivery, I will not go to the clinic and the white room they have prepared for me. For my delivery I will go to the Hermitage. I didn't tell the secondhand man. He would have stopped me. He is the representative of the continent in Oât and he sees to it that all the rules are followed. The rules say I have to go to the clinic for my delivery. I left at night without making any noise so I would not wake up the secondhand man. I didn't leave him a note, so that he might think I went to rest in the bungalow on Seagull Beach. I put my things in my bag and I took along more provisions than for my first trip, which I really did not plan very well. But I had no experience back then. With all my provisions, I am in no danger of dying of hunger. I did the right thing going to Seagull Beach on foot every Sunday. I was in practice for walking and I am in good shape physically despite my condition. I decided to take the journey to the Hermitage in short stages. I do not want to be completely worn out when I get to the falls.

I can't say how I felt when I left Oât and set out for the Hermitage. I wished I could be there already, and hear the sound of the falls again. Every night, I slept in a woodcutter's cabin. The cabins are made of a wood that stands up to the weather, not like the wood in the houses in Oât. I slept a dreamless sleep. Walking is good for me. The road is much narrower now. It's not a road anymore. It has become a path as far as the truck driver's old sawmill. The forest is taking over. After the sawmill, the path becomes a trail. The trail is well marked, as if someone was maintaining it. There are footprints. That proves there are still travelers who come up to the falls. My heart started beating very hard when I got near the Hermitage and heard the sound of the falls in the distance. I left the trail so I could follow the river. I want to come to the Hermitage by way of the river like I used to. I recognized all the rocks, all 105 the pools. Nothing has changed. The Hermitage has not changed. Everything is in order. I went back to my old room. I slept for a very long time in my old bed. I had forgotten what it was like to sleep so soundly.

As soon as I woke up, I took the sign from my bag and I put it back up over the front door just where it was before, thanks to the ladder which is still there as well, stored away where it used to be. Like before, above the front door to the Hermitage, in letters of the old alphabet, it says: Souvenir Shop. The Hermitage had to have its sign back, even if it is not a souvenir shop anymore. I reread the explanation in the pamphlet one last time. Everything is well explained. I am not afraid. This is really where I had to come for my delivery. It was a long journey, but it was not beyond my strength. The walk was undoubtedly a good preparation for the delivery. The farther up the path I climbed, the more I could feel movement in my stomach.

I spent the last day resting by the falls. I saw the rainbow again in the mist of the falls. The black quartz rocks still reflect the same strong light Rose used to talk about. It's a blinding light that hurts my eyes now that I am no longer used to it. I closed my eyes so I could hear the sound of the falls better. Suddenly I had the impression that the sound was coming up from the bottom of my stomach. Then I knew that it would be very soon.

When I felt the first pains, I put my things away in my bag and I climbed up to the grotto. I want my delivery to be in the grotto. The pains lasted all night and all morning. At noon, when the sun was at its height and came into the grotto, I was delivered. I did the whole thing without panicking, as it is explained in the pamphlet. I did every step in order, right up to the cord, which I cut myself. I managed it all alone in the grotto.

It's a little girl. I named her Rose. As soon as I saw her, I named her Rose. I bathed her where the river comes up out of the ground. The river water is warm when it comes out of the mountain. There is no danger of Rose catching a chill. She seems robust and solidly built. I wanted her first bath to be in the spring that feeds the river, like a baptism. Then I wrapped her in my bridal veil. I brought it along especially for Rose. Rose is beautiful wrapped in my bridal veil. She has the same blue eyes as Yem. I made her a little bed of sand and moss, and I laid her down in the semidarkness of the grotto with Mellie's shawl as a blanket. I brought everything I needed for Rose. She has been sleeping ever since I bathed her. I watched her sleep for a long time, and then I was so tired and worn out that I fell asleep too. There is a gentle warmth in the grotto.

When I woke up, I took Rose in my arms. I rocked her for a long time singing a song Rose used to sing to me when I was little. Rose woke up and cried. So I gave her my breast. But Rose went on crying in spite of the breast. I have no milk. Why do I have no milk? I made up a bottle of formula for her, carefully following the instructions given in the pamphlet. Rose drank all her formula. Then she went back to sleep nestled against me and I also went back to sleep nestled against her.

I spent two more days with Rose in the grotto. I feel weaker every day. I have a louder and louder buzzing in my ears. I watch Rose sleeping. I rock her and sing Rose's song. I bathe her in the warm spring that feeds the river. I give her her formula. Rose is sheltered in the grotto. Nothing bad can happen to her.

At dawn on the third day, I left the grotto. I am coming back down alone, without baggage. I gave Rose her last bottle. I wrote her name on the book of legends. I wrote on the cover of the book: FOR ROSE. I wrote it twice, in the old alphabet and in the new alphabet. My book of legends with my twelve photos inside is my gift for Rose. I put it down by her feet where it would be very visible. I am also leaving her my bag. Inside it is the empty polaroid and my jewel case. Before the delivery, I took off all my jewels and put them back in the case. That is my second gift for Rose. It's a gift from Yem as well, since Yem was the one who gave me the jewel case. I only kept the ring on my finger, the ring from my wedding with Yem. My identity card is also in the book of legends. The secondhand man had not forgotten to write the date of my marriage to Yem on it.

I put some food in my pockets, but I can't swallow anything. Fortunately the path is downhill, I only have to let myself descend. I can't feel my legs anymore, I can't even feel my body. I walk as if I were in a dream. I no longer recognize the path or the forest. In the evening, I don't have the strength to look for a cabin, so I sleep beside the path. At night, the cold makes me shiver as I lie beside the path. As soon as I started the trip down I noticed that my underwear was stained with blood. I am losing blood. It isn't the same blood as my period. The period does not start up again so soon after delivery. It must be one of those complications they explain in the pamphlet. Walking is bad for hemorrhages. The blood is flowing drop by drop without stopping. Something must be torn somewhere inside. There are drops of blood behind me on the path. Even though I am feeling weaker and weaker, I never stop. I think about Rose and the Queen of the Fairies.

I came to the crossroads. On the left is the road that leads to Oât, and on the right is the road that leads to Seagull Beach. I took the road to Seagull Beach. I turned around one last time to look at the road that climbs up to the Hermitage. That was when I saw a couple of travelers making their way along the road. Tomorrow, or maybe tonight if they walk quickly, they will come to the falls, they will climb to the grotto. They will find Rose. Maybe they will decide to move into the Hermitage and to reopen the souvenir shop now that the sign is there again?

When I reached Seagull Beach, I immediately climbed into the Buick. As soon as I lay down on the back seat, I lost consciousness. I don't know how much time went by before I came around. The back seat of the Buick is stained with blood. The blood is still flowing. It's bad to lose so much blood. What a state the Buick is in. It's all rusty and now the back seat is stained with blood. The seagulls finally tore through the top with their beaks. They invaded the Buick. They are all over the front seats, there is a flock of them squeezed up against me in the back seat, there are some on the hood looking at me through the windshield, and looking at the blood. The seagulls would be keeping me warm if I were not so cold. I am trembling with cold.

I sat up a little so I could look at the beach. The window is dirty, the ocean looks dirty through the window. I see a big white yacht anchored right in front of the Buick. I have never seen such a big yacht. I don't see anything written on the yacht. The hull is an immaculate white, without any letters painted on it. I have no way of knowing the name of the yacht. I am still losing blood. I have a veil before my eyes. The yacht is becoming more and more blurry. I call Yem's name like I used to do in the Buick. But today is not Sunday. Sunday will be my birthday, I will be sixteen. Where is Yem with the Queen of the Fairies? Did he get to the end of the channel? I would have liked so much to tell him about Rose.

The wind picked up. The yacht is sailing away from Seagull Beach. I saw it for a long time, disappearing little by little out to sea. The wind picks up the sand on the beach. There are no footprints on the sand because of the wind that erases them all. The seagulls flew off all together with one great flurry. They abandoned the Buick.

The ocean is empty, like Seagull Beach. I am alone in the Buick, all alone now that the seagulls have flown off high in the sky, far away. The sand covers the windshield and the other windows with a fine film. I can't see the beach anymore, or the ocean, or the sky, or the seagulls. The veil in front of my eyes is becoming thicker and thicker. I can't even see the blood on the seat. I can't see anything anymore, nothing but Rose wrapped in my bridal veil in the Fairy Grotto.

The Story of the Triptych

Hôtel Splendid (October–November 1985), *Forever Valley* (May–July 1986), *Rose Mellie Rose* (October–December 1986): three novels written in the space of a year, with no idea, before finishing the third, that they could be seen as a triptych, the story of my birth as a novelist after the genesis of my first three books, *Le Mort & Cie* (poetry), *Doublures* (stories), and *Tir et Lir* (drama).

As an epigraph to *Hôtel Splendid,* a sentence from Rimbaud's *Illuminations:* 'The caravans left. And the Hôtel Splendid was built in the chaos of ice and polar night.' If the triptych had any initial goal, it might have been that of delivering myself – while remaining a poet – of the curse of the great poetry of the nineteenth century, which Rimbaud foresaw brilliantly in his prophetic 'Le Bateau ivre.' How to deliver oneself of the temptation of that boat, of that obsession (which continually returns, like a ghost ship, in *Rose Mellie Rose:* Yem's *Queen of the Fairies,* the wreck of the great ship sinking into the lagoon, the white, nameless yacht that appears to Mellie at the end), if not by undertaking to build something on solid ground? Rimbaud, who did not survive his own shipwreck, nevertheless suggests in that sentence from 'After the Flood' a possible rescue, pointing the way to an escape route.

The triptych might begin, then, with the question of the great poetry of the nineteenth century, which ends tragically in the twentieth with the ruined work of Artaud. This poetry returns in the form of the Hôtel Splendid, which resembles 'a boat that has run aground on the snow with its wooden hull half rotted away.' If it were to find the answer to that question, the triptych would mark a border between what must be salvaged from that poetry and what must be reinvented in the novel. The triptych, then, is situated at a crossroads, that of a double farewell: to the poetry of the nineteenth century (which the Surrealists vainly tried to resuscitate) and to the great novel of the nineteenth century (which, after the apotheosis of Proust, explodes in the work of Céline and lies dying in that of Beckett). Like the New Novelists, I seek to begin something new, but my attempt, unlike theirs, takes place at the intersection of two histories: that of poetry and that of the novel. To build a new literature on still-virgin soil, Rimbaud's 'chaos of ice and polar night,' already explored by the brilliant surveyor Kafka, armed with his ax 'to break the frozen sea inside oneself.' Literature again conceived as the work of a pioneer, like the grandmother in *Hôtel Splendid*, who in her folly dared to build her hotel at the edge of the swamp where nothing had ever been built before. A work of civilization as well, and of progress (thus reestablishing a link with the Enlightenment), against the ruin and death of which the poetry of the nineteenth century was a bearer.

Haunted by this poetry to which it must say its farewells, the triptych tells of the threat of flood: the swamp in *Hôtel Splendid* submerging the cemetery and the embankment and constantly attacking the hotel; the underground lake tapped in order to flood Forever Valley when the dam is built; the lagoon of Oât flooding and destroying the old lagoon neighborhood. The flooding of a literature, a world, a History?

To combat this threat, it is necessary in each case to undertake a work – the work of a builder and of a historian. Every day, the narrator of *Hôtel Splendid* unblocks the lavatories, plugs the leaks in the pipes, repairs the rotting beams; every day except Saturday and Sunday, the narrator of *Forever Valley* digs her four pits at the four points of the compass around the ruined church, trying to search for the dead and to build her cemetery before the final flood. And in the course of her short life in Oât, Mellie creates her book, her twelve Polaroid photos with the legends she writes on the back, and which she puts into Rose's book of legends written in the old alphabet. But as for her house, because of Yem's departure with the *Queen of the Fairies,* she will be able to build no more than the foundation. Each of these three narrators is in a way a metaphor for the writer that I am: a writer trying to build a body of work upon the end of a literature, upon the lost utopia of a generation, upon a society in crisis, and at the same time upon a History that must be reinvented.

If the question of inheritance lies at the heart of the triptych, that is because one cannot try to rebuild without
assuming one's heritage, however heavy it may be. The
heritage of the past returns throughout the triptych, like
three phases that must be worked through: my history, the
history of women, and literature, which is also the legend-
ary history of the world. Seeking from *Le Mort & Cie*
onwards to begin a new history ('the dwarf leaves / the
kingdom / with his empty satchel'), I was forced to pass
through all the old lost history again. Lost at the very
bottom of my memory, this history could only be written
as fiction. But here fiction is not an escape into the unreal;
on the contrary, it is the only way to recapture the reality
of the history that had been lost.

As there are three books, there are three heritages. First
the grandmother's legacy, the half-rotted Hôtel Splendid
that the narrator will rescue from death by making of it
her own hotel, the Splendid, which resembles no other:
'Thanks to grandmother's enterprising spirit, this is the
only swamp with a hotel in the entire region. The Splendid is visible from everywhere in the swamp. Its signs
shine at night, they are visible from a great distance. There
are two bright spots in the sky and on the snow. They are
the reflections of the Splendid's signs.'

In the central panel of the triptych, the legacy of Forever Valley (left by the father and the mayor, thus by the
Fathers) is nothing more than ruins, loss, and death. The
narrator of *Forever Valley* is the only one of the three to

have no inheritance, other than her rootedness in the place and in its name. It is no coincidence that she can neither read nor write, and that she is not developed. Her only way out, her 'personal project,' is to look for the dead: to take on the work of an archaeologist and a historian, in search of the traces of a lost heritage. And also the work of a builder, since she builds the cemetery that the ruined hamlet lacks. She will not find the dead, but she will uncover the deadly geology of the site: a vein of sludge that crosses a ridge of stone. And in place of the dead that she never finds, she will bury her own dead (the father, who passed nothing down to her, and Bob, the never-to-be fiancé), thus becoming the gravedigger for a lost past and a doomed present. The cemetery reappears throughout the triptych – and beyond – because there is a vital need to bury the dead in order to be delivered of them, in order to say farewell to them, to save their memory, the memory of names, the epitaphs on the gravestones.

The narrator of *Forever Valley* is the first to leave her place of origin. But she will be unable to live in the valley below, unable to detach herself from Forever Valley. 'Bob had a lesion. I can get along with anemia.' None of the three narrators of the triptych will find a way out through a departure. The narrator of *Hôtel Splendid* can only live in her hotel; the narrator of *Forever Valley* cannot live in the valley below; Mellie refuses to leave Oât and goes away to die alone on Seagull Beach, just as Yem went away to lose himself in the channel. The weight of the heritage (or of its absence), its power of love and death, is too great for the heroine to free herself of it. She can only use her will to live and to find an identity for herself as a means of transforming the heritage, making of it a work.

The end of the triptych, however, opens onto another story. If Mellie dies, it is only after having given life to Rose, to whom she will pass down her own inheritance, now metamorphosed. Mellie, the only narrator of the triptych to bear a name, has as her task not only the transformation of her heritage into a work (like the first two narrators), but also the transmission of that heritage to Rose, thus opening up the story to another time, that of the reality of the world and the possibility of love. Like the first narrator, Mellie inherits something (from Rose, her adoptive mother), but Mellie's inheritance is not cursed. It is a sort of treasure: the book of legends in the old alphabet, the book from which she learned to read, a book of myths and poetry, a fairy-tale book passed down by women. But this treasure, like the sign of the Hermitage, is ill-suited to the world Mellie lives in after Rose's death. She is the first narrator to move away from her place of origin (although the seaport of Oât is a part of that same island, which bears its name). On her own in Oât, she will find her identity, she will have an identity card, she will learn the new alphabet, earn her certificate by correspondence, find work in the municipal offices, have her sexual initiation at the tea dances of the Continental, become engaged and married to Yem, and then bring Rose into the world. And from this life that she lived as thoroughly as she could, from her very singular inheritance, she creates her book – her twelve photos that tell in the manner of a poem the story of her life in Oât – a book that she leaves, along with the old book, to Rose. 'I wrote her name on the book of legends. I wrote it twice, in the old alphabet and in the new alphabet. My book of legends is my gift for Rose.' To this book, which is now two books, she adds her identity card, and next to it her bag, along with her empty Polaroid and her jewel case. 'That is my second gift for Rose. It is a gift from Yem as well, since Yem was the one who gave me the jewel case.' With this new legacy, Mellie makes possible for Rose a story that will be different from her own, even if this story begins in the same way. Abandoned by Mellie in the grotto just as Mellie had been, Rose will be cared for by the couple Mellie sees climbing toward the Hermitage at the end.

Another element of the profound unity of the triptych is the voice of the narrator, at the same time heroine and storyteller. A voice born of a natural environment which brings first death (the swamp in *Hôtel Splendid,* the sterile mountains of *Forever Valley*) and then life (the grotto and the falls of the Hermitage). And each site holds the last vestiges of a civilization (a sick hotel, a ruined hamlet, a souvenir shop that closes). In this duality of the site the voice finds its singular language: at the same time elementary and poetic, the language of the origin, of myths and legends, but also the amnesic language of the end of the world, of which there remains only the basic lexical and syntactic structure. Each time, however, these lost sites are linked to the modern world (the railway company of *Hôtel Splendid*, the valley below in *Forever Valley*, the continent in *Rose Mellie Rose*). It is toward this modern world that the narrator, starting in *Forever Valley*, will have to move. In Oât, Mellie learns the new alphabet and earns her certificate. The ancient language of the book of legends and the amnesic language of the father's closed book are grafted onto the language of education and modernity, thus becoming socialized and allowing communication. It is in a way from these three languages that I may have invented my language as a writer. The emptiness and strangeness of this language may also have allowed me to bring about in it a richness which is not that of the grand style of French literature. A woman's language as well, no doubt, which allowed me to put forth a new system of imagination, in which the image created by the fiction is in a sense projected onto the emptiness created in the language.

Voices that recount the lost history of women: Ada and Adel, the cursed sisters of the Splendid; Massi, the widow of the mayor of Forever Valley; Miss Martha, the former teacher of Oât who becomes deputy mayor, only to end up tragically at the Dance Palace. Women who live in madness and death, or in an alienating identification with a conquering modernity. The narrators alone are figures of the emancipation of women: they are the ones who fight, who build, who seek, who pass down a work.

If the narrators become younger and more feminine from book to book, that is because the triptych is also a search for femininity. Moving from *Hôtel Splendid*'s asexual narrator – whose only libidinal attachment is to her hotel, her lavatories, and her pipes – to the undeveloped sixteen-year-old narrator of *Forever Valley*, condemned to prostitution in Massi's dancehall and an impossible love for Bob, the probationary customs officer, we finally come to Mellie, whose story begins on her twelfth birthday (which is also the day of her first period and of her sexual initiation with the truck driver) and ends when she is sixteen, when she gives birth to Rose. The history of a lost, mutilated, and prostituted femininity, which from one book to the next tries to win itself back by reinventing itself.

This history returns to pose the question of love, passing back through the old myths linked to death (the narrator of *Forever Valley*, as well as Bob, Yem, and Mellie), myths to which we must also say our goodbyes. Historically linked to the moment at which women gained their emancipation and at which the old utopias died, the triptych seeks both to say farewell to an entire history and to save the part of that history that must not die, but which must be rewritten in another way: poetry, myth, utopia, love.

The anamnesis of a lost history, the triptych is also a progressive opening-up to the historical present, which makes itself felt a little more clearly with each book. If in *Hôtel Splendid* the railway company fails to build the embankment across the swamp, the valley below succeeds in building the dam that will drown Forever Valley, while in *Rose Mellie Rose* the all-powerful continent gradually empties and conquers Oât, which survives only through the museum, the souvenir shop, and the secondhand man's shop. It is in this new world – which has little by little conquered the old – that the triptych ends, just as it ends with Rose's new heritage, thus opening the way for the writing of a new story, that of the present time and the present world.

Marie Redonnet

In the European Women Writers Series